SALT SCRUBS & STRANGERS

A COZY SPA MYSTERY~ BOOK 8

JENN COWAN

JRC PRESS

1
———

"Autumn, I think I found the guy who the captain hired..." Travis's voice trails off as he takes in the scene. "Am I interrupting something?"

I smile and hold up a gloved hand with salt on it. "Um, kind of. We're in the middle of a class on salt scrubs."

"Mrs. Parker, is this something that can wait?" Instructor Tony Soggs asks, sticking his thin nose up in the air as he eyes Travis with contempt.

"We have a break in about fifteen minutes. Cat's in the break room if you wouldn't mind waiting in there for me until I'm done?" I ask, trying not to roll my eyes at the pretentious instructor.

Travis shoots the instructor a stern look before nodding to me and heading back to the break room.

"Now, if there aren't going to be any further interruptions." He glares at me before turning toward another couple. "Take the hot towels and wipe down your client. Be sure to use long strokes and get off as much salt as you can. For those of you who are serious about adding salt scrubs to your services, I highly recommend getting a Vishy shower installed." He shoots me another pointed look. "Hot towels will only get off so much salt then your client will have to go home and shower. It's not an ideal solution." He sighs dramatically. "But it will have to do for now."

I grab a towel from the hot towel cabi and begin wiping down my partner, Olive Young's slender back as the instructor starts critiquing another student's technique. He's been critical of everything since he walked into the spa. The lights are too bright. The tables are too narrow. The space isn't big enough. Our techniques aren't smooth. Like there's a certain way to apply salt scrub to the body or wipe it off. I mean seriously this guy is just looking for something to complain about. A headache's forming at the back of my skull and five o'clock can't get here soon enough. Not to mention, this is only the first day. There are still two more days of this stuff. I force a smile at Instructor Soggs, as he wants to be called, when he walks by and continue wiping the towel over my partner's back.

"Ow! Um, Autumn, not so hard," Olive whisper-yells, lifting her head from the face rest and swiping her black curls from her face.

"Oh, sorry." I slow my strokes and curb the urge to fling the towel at the instructor as he berates another student for their poor technique.

Olive scowls at him. "What's his problem? We've all paid good money to be here and learn, not to mention this class has been rescheduled what twelve times?"

"Thirteen." I sigh. "Between the snow and conflicting schedules, it's like someone didn't want this class to happen."

Olive snorts. "Then he schedules it on Father's Day weekend. Who does that?"

"Did you have plans?"

She shakes her head. "No, but anything would have been better than lying here being yelled at and treated like we're kindergarteners."

I smirk. "Kindergarteners would eat him alive."

She giggles.

"What's so funny, Miss Young? Is Mrs. Parker a comedian, now?" He hurries over to my table and sneers down at me. "Maybe you should change professions and do stand up. Care to share the joke with the rest of the class." Instructor Soggs sweeps his arm out and gestures to the other four therapists in the room.

I shake my head and grab another towel from the towel cabi. I can feel his beady eyes on me, but I'm thankful he moves on.

"Once you're finished getting all the salt off your partner." He lets out an exasperated breath then adds, "The best you can, given the circumstances, those of you on the tables may get dressed then all of you can take a fifteen-minute break. We still have a lot to cover in the next hour and a half."

Muttering comes from the other class members then the therapists on the tables grab their robes and head toward various treatment rooms to get dressed. I throw the wet towels into laundry bin and wipe down the table before fleeing to the break room.

Travis and Cat are sitting on the couch talking. They look up when I come in the room.

"How's it going?" Cat pops up from her seat and hurries to the stove to grab the tea kettle.

I groan softly and roll my eyes.

"That good, huh," Travis says with a smirk. "I know all the snow we got this winter and even this spring made it hard to get this class in, but I figured you would have just cancelled it by now."

I sigh and plop down in one of the chairs around the table. "I need the hours for my license and so do some of the other therapists."

"You could have taken another course. Maybe an online one?"

"Josh scheduled this before he died. It was the last thing he did for me. I couldn't cancel it." I rub my temples to ward off the growing headache.

Travis studies me with a frown. "I'm sure Josh would have understood. You've been under a lot of stress lately with running this business by yourself. Now, you're hosting this class. I'm worried about you. You're pushing yourself too hard."

I shoot him an appreciative smile. "I could say the same for you," I counter, raising an eyebrow at him.

He shrugs. "It's not like I have much of a choice. I'm the interim captain until the council figures out what they're going to do."

"Still, I'm worried about you. You're pushing yourself too hard," I mimic back to him.

"Really mature, Aut," he says, rolling his eyes.

I stiffen at his nickname for me and think of Lindy's vision. Travis and I getting married and having twins. Does he think we're just going to pick up where we left off in high school? Is he expecting us to start dating right away? We haven't really talked in the past few months. We've both been busy not to mention, I've been avoiding him because I'm not sure what to do or say around him. I'm not sure what my feelings are for him. I buried those feeling because I was married to Josh. In love with Josh. Just thinking about Josh makes my heart ache. It's been almost seven months since he was murde..." I gulp down the bile rising in my throat then remember why Travis is here. "You found the guy... the one who the captain hired to ki-kill Josh?" I swallow again to keep from vomiting.

Travis studies me for a moment like he's trying to read my mind and decide where my head is before saying, "I think so. An auto shop in Villsboro reported a guy came in yesterday with front end damage to a truck that matches the description of the one involved in the accident."

I snort. "It was no accident. The guy purposely ran over my husband because the captain paid him or blackmailed him, who knows, but he purposely killed my husband."

"Speaking of the captain, he's denying any involvement in Josh's death. He's still saying it was simply an unfortunate accident," Travis says, standing up and coming over to the table to sit down next to me.

"He's lying," I scoff. "He looked me right in the eye and told me I was going to pay for putting my nose in all his cases then I immediately find out about Josh's accident. He was behind it. I just know it."

Travis reaches out and places his hand over mine. "I'm doing everything in my power to get to the bottom of it while keeping it on the down low. I don't want to upset the Parkers by investigating their son's death. They think it was an accident and that he died a hero." He pauses and studies me for a moment before adding, "I'm glad they're still in Florida with your parents. It will make it easier to look into this without them getting wind of anything."

I nod and stare down at his hand on mine. I quickly move away and tuck a strand of hair behind my ear. Travis's hand on mine just feels wrong. I feel like I'm cheating on my husband even though Josh gave me his blessing to move on and specifically with Travis. I just can't. Not yet. I fiddle with my left ring finger, which is bare because I took my rings off to participate in this class. It feels weird without them on. I haven't had the heart to put them away in my jewelry box. I thought about putting them on a gold chain around my neck, but even that feels wrong. I've had Josh's wedding band resized and I wear it on my right ring finger. It makes me feel closer to him.

"Here's your tea, Autumn," Cat says, setting a cup of chamomile in front of me.

"Thanks, sweetie." I smile up at her and take a sip of tea, not risking a glance at Travis.

He clears his throat and leans back in his chair. "I was going to take a drive up to the shop tonight. Do you want to come with me?"

"Um." I chew on my lip debating my options.

"When will this class be over?"

"Um, around five."

"I can grab a pizza and we can drive up to Villsboro when you're done."

My stomach churns thinking about being alone with Travis. Will he want to talk about our relationship? Is he considering this a date? I take another sip of tea to calm my nerves.

"Mrs. Parker, if you care to join us, we need to get started," Instructor Soggs calls from the other room.

I sigh and stand up.

"Autumn, do you want to go with me tonight?" Travis inquires again with a frown on his face.

I chew on my lower lip again, not sure what to do.

"Can I go too?" Cat inquires, picking up on my uncertainty.

"That would be great," I pipe up before Travis can tell her it's too dangerous. "Why don't you help your dad pick out some salads too? I'll meet you guys out front a little after five." I hurry out of the room before Travis can veto my plans and before I chicken out.

2

───────

My head's throbbing as I step out into the warm night. It's a little after five and thankfully, Instructor Soggs let out class a little early. It gave me a chance to clean up before I have to meet up with Travis and Cat.

Class was brutal. Instructor Soggs yelled at each of us no matter what we did, it was never good enough. I'm not sure I can take two more days of this. It's not like there's a lot more he can teach us about salt scrubs, but he indicates there's more to learn.

"Autumn, over here." Cat waves from the backseat of the SUV.

I lock the spa door and head over to them.

Travis gets out and opens the door for me.

I refuse to meet his eyes, muttering my thanks as I slip into the passenger seat. The car smells of cooked dough and tomato sauce.

"Here's your salad," Cat says, handing me a plastic bowl.

"Thanks, hun." I take it and open the lid. It's my favorite veggie salad yet I don't really have an appetite. I pick around at my salad as Travis pulls onto the road leading to Villsboro.

"How was class?" Travis asks, keeping his eyes fixed on the road.

I groan and take a bite of salad.

He chuckles. "Is it going to go all weekend?"

"Unfortunately, yes."

"Did you have other plans for this weekend? Cat said you had it marked out."

I swallow the spinach in my mouth and whisper, "I was going to spread Josh's ashes in the woods behind my house."

No one says anything for a few minutes then Cat chimes in. "We could go with you on Sunday after class. It gets done around three, right?"

"It does, but I think I need to do this alone. Thanks for offering though." I turn around and smile at her.

She gives me a sad smile in return then digs into her salad.

We eat in silence for a while then Travis says, "When we get to the shop, I want you to wait in the car, okay Cat?"

"Ookayy," Cat mumbles through a mouth full of food.

Travis slides his green eyes toward me. "You can wait in the car too if this is going to be too hard for you."

I shake my head and swallow the lump in my throat. "I'll be fine." My stomach churns and I'm not sure I can eat anymore. I place the lid on the salad bowl and set it on the floor board.

"How are you, Autumn?" Travis asks, glancing over at me briefly before focusing back on the road.

"I'm fine," I declare, clasping my hands in my lap.

"Aut, it's me. You don't have to pretend."

I fidget with my hands then realize I forgot to put on my wedding rings. Panic fills me, trying to remember where I put them. Then I remember they're locked inside the desk in the office. I put them in the drawer before class. Sighing, I lean back against the seat and close my eyes.

"Have you thought about talking to someone? I highly recommend the counselor I saw after my accident," Travis offers, reaching over and grasping my hand.

My eyes fly open at his touch and I squirm away from him.

He frowns, but doesn't say anything as he returns his hand to the wheel.

I try not to feel guilty about it, but I feel like every time Travis touches me, I'm cheating on my husband... my dead husband. It's not like Josh and I got a divorce. He was taken from me. Way too soon. We were newlyweds and should have had our whole lives together. It's not fair. "I'm sorry," I mutter to Travis.

"For what?" He shrugs as if it's no big deal.

I purse my lips and give him a look that says he knows exactly what I'm talking about.

"Autumn," he starts and glances in the rearview mirror to check on Cat, who has her earbuds in and is jamming out to her playlist. "We don't have to rush anything. I'm your friend. First and foremost. We don't have to be anything more until you're ready. I'm not going anywhere. I'll take you as my friend. My girlfriend. My wife... hopefully." He shoots me a grin.

"What if I'm never ready?" I ask, quietly, toying with my bare ring finger. It feels so naked without Josh's rings on it. I tried to give his mother back the engagement ring since it's a family heirloom, but she wouldn't hear of it.

His smile falters, but he recovers quickly. "Like I said, there's no rush. We can take it a day at a time. It's only been seven months. You can't flip a switch and turn off those feelings and turn on the ones for me. I still have a lot to prove to you."

"You do?"

Travis nods. "I betrayed you. I cheated on you because my ego got in the way when I was an insecure teenager. I'm not that boy anymore. I've grown up if you haven't noticed." He wiggles his eyebrows at me, making me laugh then his expression turns serious. "I want to prove to you that I will never do anything to hurt you or give you any reason not to trust me." He pauses for a moment then says softly, "I love you, Autumn. I always have and I always will. Time hasn't changed my feelings for you. If anything, it's made them stronger and made me realize there's no one else for me. Only you. It's always been you... and it always will be."

Tears are falling down my cheeks before I even realize it. I swipe them away and swallow down the massive lump in my throat.

"Autumn? You're crying. Why are you crying? Dad, what did you say to her?" Cat leans forward in her seat and slugs her father in the arm before squeezing my shoulder.

Travis chuckles and shakes his head. "I guess I know who's side you're on," he teases Cat, trying to lighten the mood.

I pat Cat's hand. "Your dad didn't say anything wrong. It was perfect."

Travis's eyebrows hit his hairline and he pulls to the side of the road to gawk at me.

I give him a small smile and tuck a strand of hair behind my ear, feeling my face grow hot.

"What did he say?" Cat sticks her head in between us and gives me her full attention.

Travis snaps out of his trance and tickles her neck. "It's private. Go back to listening to your songs."

Cat giggles and flops back in her seat. "Fine, don't tell me, but I'll find out eventually."

"Fat chance," Travis retorts then winks at me before steering the car back on the road.

We ride in silence for a little bit while I think about everything Travis said to me. His words were perfect. It was everything I've ever wanted to hear from him. I guess I've been living in fear. Fear of loving him only for him to crush me again. I barely survived the first betrayal, I know I couldn't bear another one. It would kill me. I think of Josh's letter and his words about how Travis knows what it's like to live without me and how he would never make that mistake again. If Josh thought giving Travis a second chance was a good idea then I need to at least be open to it, right?

"There's the auto shop." Travis points to a rundown brick building with a high chain link fence around it. A sign that reads, "Frank's Auto Shop" is hanging from the fence and a couple of pit bulls are barking their heads off at us.

"Ah, they're so cute," Cat coos at the dogs.

"Cat, stay in the car," Travis orders sternly. "It's their job is to protect the auto shop."

"But they're so sweet. You worry too much, Dad."

I quirk an eyebrow because the dogs look ready to pounce on Travis as soon as he opens the door.

Cat cracks the window and begins baby talking to them.

The dogs quiet down and move toward her door. They wag their tails and sit when she tells them to.

Travis shoots me a perplexed look then shakes his head and steps slowly out of the car.

"Tank. Shooter, come," a harsh voice barks from the auto shop.

The dogs give Cat one last tail wag before running over to their owner, who I assume is Frank.

"Please stay in the car," I reiterate to Cat before opening my door and stepping out into the humid night air. I'm already starting to sweat as I make my way over to Travis. He's waiting for me at the hood of the car with his hand on his gun. He seems on high alert and is scanning the area.

"You Detective Mills?" an old man in gray coveralls with greasy gray hair and a shaggy beard asks, limping over to us.

"I am and I'm assuming you're Frank Peterson?" Travis extends his hand to the man.

"Yes, sir." He moves his beady brown eyes from Travis to me. "And who is this beauty?"

Travis stiffens next to me, he's always hated when another man compliments me, even if they're senior citizens.

I stick my hand out to him. "Autumn Parker."

He nods and takes my hand. "It's a pleasure. What's a pretty little thing like you doing out here? Shouldn't you be home with your husband? Or is this your husband and you kept your maiden name? Some ladies do that now."

I blink back the tears forming in my eyes and choke out, "My husband's dead."

"Oh, my condolences," he says, then kisses the back of my hand.

Travis clears his throat and moves to break the contact between me and Frank. "You said on the phone that you had a truck with front end damage and blood in the headlights."

I stiffen at the mention of blood... what if it's Josh's blood? I sway slightly.

Travis must have felt the movement because he reaches out to steady me. "You can wait in the car while I check out the truck and take some samples."

I shake my head and gulp back the bile in my throat. "No, I'm fine."

"You're her, aren't you?" Frank studies me like I'm a foreign specimen.

"Who?" I inquire stepping closer to Travis because I'm feeling light-headed and, if I'm being honest, to find comfort in his presence. His woodsy cologne has always been calming to me. It's like walking through a forest of pine trees.

"You're that sleuth from Daysville. The one whose husband was hit by a truck several months ago. Parker. It was Josh Parker. You're his wife."

Travis interjects before I can answer, "Mr. Peterson, it's getting late and we would like to see the truck. Mrs. Parker's here as a consultant for the police department."

Frank nods slowly then motions for us to follow him to the shop. The dogs are eating their dinner by the bay door when he raises it up and gestures to the truck sitting inside. "There she is. Pretty nice truck, but it needs a lot of body work as you can see."

The entire front end is completely smashed in. There's blood caked on the broken headlights and hair particles are sticking out of them. I swallow down the salad threatening to make a reappearance.

Travis walks around the truck to inspect it from all angles. "Did the guy say what he hit?"

"A deer."

"But you didn't think so? I'm assuming that's why you called me."

Frank nods. "I heard about that hit and run so I've been keeping an eye out for any trucks with front end damage. This is the only one I've seen so far. I thought it was better to have it checked out then to regret it later. I'm surprised the guy was dumb enough to stay around these parts. I would have hightailed it out of state and ditched the truck."

Travis bends down and plucks some hair from the head-light and puts them in an evidence baggy. Then he takes out his phone and snaps some pictures of the damage and the license plate. "How long will it take to fix?"

"I told the guy at least a week, but I can extend it if you need me to."

Travis opens the passenger side door and grabs the registration out of the glove box. "Daniel Myers. He's from Villsboro. Do you know him?"

Frank nods. "Unfortunately, I do. Danny's a regular in the bars and has been arrested for petty crimes on numerous occasions. I heard he got himself in some trouble there in Daysville last fall. Something about some under-ground gambling ring. Owed a guy a bunch of money."

Travis exchanges a knowing glance with me. "Well thank you for calling. I'll have the lab run these hair samples and I'll be in touch if I need you to postpone the repairs."

"Of course, Detective." Then Frank turns to me and gives me a sympathetic smile. "I'm sorry about your husband. I hope you get the closure you're searching for."

"Thank you," I whisper as I turn to head back to Travis's SUV.

Travis opens my door. "You okay?"

"No," I say, glancing back at the damaged truck before Frank closes the door. "I won't be until this guy is caught and the captain... ex-captain pays for what he's done."

Travis squeezes my shoulder. "He will. I won't stop until we get justice for Josh. I promise you." He pauses then opens his mouth to say something else when his radio goes off, "All units to the Daysville Bed and Breakfast."

3

"What happened?" I ask, stepping into the parlor room of the bed and breakfast.

"Oh, Autumn, it's awful," Olive cries, flinging her arms around my neck.

I pat her back and glance around the room at the solemn faces of the strangers I met just today. Anita and George Case are sitting next to each other on the couch. Both of them blond and thin wearing their scrubs from earlier. They just got married last month and run a spa together in Colorado.

Sloan Burke is standing by the fireplace staring at a non-existent fire. He runs a hand through his dark hair then meets my eyes, but quickly turns away. His stocky frame hugs his black scrubs, making them look almost too small for him. Supposedly, he owns a sports medicine clinic in Arkansas so why he's here for a salt scrub course, I'm not sure.

Paula Arnold's sitting in the window seat staring out into the night. She's changed out of her scrubs into tie dye yoga pants and a low-cut blue sweater pushed up to her elbows revealing an array of colorful tattoos on her forearms. Her long rose-colored hair hangs in waves down her back. She hasn't been very friendly toward me or anyone for that matter. I haven't gotten her whole story yet, but I can tell there is one. Her Arkansas spa is small, but from what I hear does well.

"Autumn, can I see you for a moment?" Travis asks, stepping into the room.

Paula's almost immediately at his side. I've never seen anyone move so quickly. "Oh, you must be the detective from earlier." She runs a rose-colored nail down his arm.

Travis frowns as he looks down at her hand on his arm. "I am. If you would please have a seat, an officer will be in to question you shortly."

"I would prefer a private questioning session with you," she coos, leaning in closer and giving Travis a full view of her chest.

I smirk and roll my eyes.

Travis meets my eyes and lifts an eyebrow as if to ask for help.

I sigh and extract myself from Olive. Once I get her settled back on the couch, I move toward Travis to rescue him. "Excuse us, Paula. We really do need to get back to the investigation." I give her a closed-lipped smile.

She narrows her eyes at me. "We? I thought you were a massage therapist, not a cop," she sneers, looking down her nose at me.

"She's a consultant for the police department. Autumn's helped with several cases over the past couple of years. All of them which she's solved." Travis beams down at me then places a hand on my lower back to guide me out of the room without another word to Paula, who looks about ready to murder me.

"It seems you have an admirer, Detective," I tease, stepping into the kitchen.

"There's only one woman I want admiring me and it definitely isn't that one," he mutters, running a hand through his red hair.

My heart flutters at his words, but I tap it down because I'm not ready to go there yet with Travis. "What do we have, Detective?"

"It seems your instructor took a tumble down the back stairs and broke his neck," Travis says, gesturing to the other side of the room where a couple of officers are taping off the scene and taking photos.

I step around the large granite top island to see the outline of Instructor Soggs's body at the bottom of the steps. "Where is he?"

"The ambulance came to get him when your friend Olive found him, but it was too late. He died instantly."

"So, it was an accident?"

"You tell me," he lifts an eyebrow at me.

I lower my voice. "You want me to see if I can see anything, don't you?"

He shrugs. "I thought it was at least worth a shot. You solved the last case with touching Lindy's journal, maybe touching the spot where he died will spark something."

I furrow my brows and stare at the body outline. "I'm not sure it works like that."

"Only one way to find out," Travis says, gently pushing me toward the stairs. "Gentlemen, can you give us a minute please?"

The officers stop what they're doing and step away from the scene.

"Thank you. Would you mind heading into the living room to begin questioning the guests?"

They nod and leave the kitchen.

I take a deep breath and crouch down in front of the body outline. There's a pool of blood at the base of the steps that hasn't been cleaned up yet so I avoid that area. I place a hand on the yellow outline and close my eyes.

"Anything?" Travis asks, squatting down next to me.

I shake my head. "Nothing. Maybe I should be at the top of the stairs where he fell."

Travis nods. "Just step carefully around the blood. I'll be right behind you."

I brace myself against the narrow staircase. There's not much room to move as I make my way up the stairs and around a small bend until I reach the second floor. "The instructor was a big man, I'm surprised he would even use these stairs," I comment as I watch Travis struggle to get through the small opening of the stairs.

"He was smaller than me, but I see what you mean. It does seem strange that he would use these stairs and not the main staircase."

I study the opening of the stairs, not exactly sure what I'm hoping to find. "What's that?" I move toward the trim of the doorway.

"What?" Travis asks, looking over my shoulder.

His warm breath tickles the back of my neck and his chest presses against my back. I gulp trying to not let his presence affect me and focus on what I found. "There's a piece of black material stuck on one of the nails." I point to the fabric and turn my head ever so slightly to look at Travis. Our eyes lock and my heart starts to thump loudly in my chest. He leans in, his eyes bouncing from my eyes to my lips as if asking permission.

Someone coughs behind us and we jerk apart.

My body feels like it's on fire and I know my face has to

match my hair. I take a deep breath to calm my racing heart and peek around Travis to see who interrupted what would have been a mistake... right? Kissing Travis is a mistake... I think?

Mr. Gillman, the old inn keeper chuckles as he moves toward the bathroom with a plunger in his wrinkled hand. "Ah to be young and in love." He's wearing khaki pants with a green and white polo. His gray hair is thinning at the top of his head and he looks like he's aged twenty years since I saw him a few months ago. Rumor has it, his sister going to jail has been hard on him. He's having to run the bed and breakfast all by himself and just doesn't have it in him to do it anymore. "This old toilet keeps getting clogged."

"Let me help you with that, Mr. Gillman," Travis offers, taking the plunger from him and stepping into the bathroom.

"Thank you, son," he says, leaning back against the door frame to watch Travis unclog the toilet.

"Mr. Gillman, how are you?"

"Oh, you know, okay. This old place is getting more and more expensive to run. I'm tempted to cut my loses and leave town." He lets out an exaggerated breath. "Now someone fell down the stairs. I'm sure there'll be a lawsuit." He shakes his head and slumps his shoulders as if defeated.

"Did they though?" I inquire, turning back to the piece of fabric at the top of the stairs. "I know these steps are narrow, but they don't seem very slick."

"Oh, they're not, but someone who isn't used to them could easily fall down them."

"Really? Has anyone ever fallen down them before?"

Mr. Gillman frowns and scratches his head. "Well, no."

"Where were you at the time of the alleged accident?"

"Alleged? Are you thinking this is murder?" Mr. Gillman's brown eyes grow wide.

"We're not ruling anything out at this point."

"Um, ok. Well I was downstairs in the den."

"Was anyone in the den with you?"

"No. That sweet couple, what's their names… oh yes, the Cases had just grabbed a couple of books and went upstairs before I heard Olive scream."

"Do you know where Paula and Sloan were?"

"Who?" He furrows his bushy brow for a moment before the names register with him. "Oh, right the other two guests. Not very friendly those two. They retreated to their rooms shortly after dinner."

"And where was Olive and Mr. Soggs?"

He strokes his chin then says, "I think in the kitchen."

"Hmm. Well thank you for your help, Mr. Gillman."

Travis comes out of the bathroom and hands Mr. Gillman the plunger. "It's all clear."

"Thank you, Detective." Mr. Gillman says with a sigh. "Well I better get back to it. Always things to fix. Repairs to make. Night you two." He waves then shuffles off to the hall closet.

"Did you get any information from Mr. Gillman?" Travis asks as we turn back to the stairs.

"A little bit," I respond then point to the black fabric. "It's a piece off someone's scrubs and unless Instructor Soggs changed clothes, he wasn't wearing black scrubs today. His were maroon." I pause and think about the massage therapists sitting in the den. "Paula's the only one not wearing her scrubs and Mr. Gillman said she didn't come down for dinner and was upstairs when the instructor took his fall. We should go talk to her." I start for the other staircase that leads to the den.

Travis grabs my arm and pulls me into him before taking a step back to distance himself from me. "Hold on, Aut. You can't just run down there and accuse her of pushing the instructor down the stairs. Let's take this piece of fabric and send it off to the lab."

I cross my arms and pout like I'm a four-year-old not getting her way.

Travis chuckles. "I'll talk to her, but we need to do this by the book. I'm not sure how I'm going to keep them all here until I can prove this is a murder. I'm assuming your class is cancelled since you no longer have an instructor."

I frown at his words then suddenly have an idea. "Maybe not."

4

____

"Autumn, what are we doing here? We have no instructor so what's the point in even being here? Especially this early on a Saturday." Paula whines into her coffee cup before plopping down on one of the massage tables.

"Regina's a cosmetologist. She's trained in body wraps, scrubs, polishes, basically everything that we were going to learn this weekend. She's also a certified instructor. This way we don't have to cancel the class and can still get our credits."

Olive steps forward and tugs on my arm to pull me to the side. "Don't you think this is a little insensitive, Autumn? I mean the instructor died last night." Tears form in her eyes and she blinks them away.

I pat her hand. "I know and I'm sorry for that, but some therapists need these CEU's to keep their license active." I don't mention that it's me who really needs these continuing education units to keep my license. These past two years I've been so busy with solving murders, I haven't had a chance to take any classes. I pause and smile. Josh knew this, which is why he booked it. My heart aches thinking about him, but I push it down and focus back on what Regina's saying to the class.

"I was able to obtain the instructors notes for the class and it looks like he was planning to teach you different ways to make your own salt scrubs. I have the supplies set up in the break room so please break into groups and head that way," Regina says, motioning toward the back of the spa. Her red hair looks like ball of fire on her head today. She added some gold highlights and has it pulled up in a messy bun. Her black smock is covering black yoga pants and a teal tunic. She tucks her arm in mine once Olive takes off toward the break room. "How are you holding up this weekend?"

I shrug and force a smile. "It's hard, but I'm fine."

She raises a perfectly plucked eyebrow at me. "Cat told me about the awkward car ride to Villsboro last night."

I jerk back slightly because I thought Cat was listening to music the whole way.

Regina chuckles. "She's a sneaky one and is determined to make you her mom."

"Her mom?" I swallow down the lump in my throat because I want to be her mom too and a mom to the babies Lindy saw in her vision. How can I though? Josh just died not even a year ago. I can't be thinking about moving on. Not yet. It just doesn't feel right. "I can't. It's too soon."

Regina pats my hand. "No one's rushing you, dear. We're here for you. To support you. Even Travis. He doesn't have any expectations for you two."

Now it's my turn to raise an eyebrow.

Regina smirks. "Well he does, but he's trying to hold back and not push you. He told me about Lindy's vision. I can't say it doesn't make me happy. Twins. Can you imagine those cute little red headed babies? Oh, I can't wait to squeeze their little cheeks and spoil them rotten."

I stiffen at her words and she notices.

"Relax, Autumn. I'm getting ahead of myself. I'm sorry. It's just there hasn't been a baby in our family for sixteen years and we didn't get to see all that much of Cat when she was a baby. April kept her away from Travis more than she let him be a part of raising her. It was so sad especially when Travis wanted so badly to be in Cat's life."

"He's a great dad."

"And he will be to your babies too and an even better husband. There's no way he would ever hurt you again, Autumn. He loves you too much. He's never stopped. I'm not saying you have to start dating today, but when you're ready, he'll definitely be waiting. Don't overthink it. He's all in for the rest of his life." She pats my hand and heads over to the table.

I take a deep breath and push away Regina's words so I can focus on this class. Thinking about me and Travis is confusing and I can't deal with it right now. I head over to Olive's table. She's smelling some essential oils while Sloan's drumming his fingers on the table like he's completely bored. "You guys ready to make some salt scrubs?"

Sloan shrugs indifferently, but Olive exclaims excitedly, "Yes. I can't wait. I've been looking forward to this part. I want to make my own line and sell it in my spa."

"That's a great idea. What about you Sloan? Are you planning to sell any salt scrubs in your office?"

He shakes his head, not meeting my eyes.

I frown because he hasn't really said much since the class started. He was quiet yesterday and barely said two words to anyone. I'm not sure how I'm going to get any information about what happened last night if he won't talk to me. I force myself to listen to what Regina's telling us and begin to mix the salt and oils. When I reach for the lavender, Sloan does too. Our hands meet and it's like a video begins to play in my mind and I see him fighting with the instructor at the top of the stairs. The same stairs the instructor fell down.

He jerks his hand away and glares at me.

I clear my throat and go back to mixing the scrub. "Did you know the instructor, Sloan?"

He grunts, but doesn't answer.

Olive gives me a strange look, but doesn't say anything.

I have to think of some way to bring up the vision I saw. It seems strange he would be fighting with the instructor. I mean Instructor Soggs wasn't very nice, but the fight seemed personal so they had to know each other prior to this class. "How did you find out about this class?"

Sloan raises an eyebrow at me. "What's with all the questions?"

"Just making conversation. I thought we could all get to know each other better."

He snorts. "What's the point? We all leave tomorrow."

"It's always nice to have friends in other places. Colleagues to refer clients to. We get a lot of tourists through our town, who ask about other spas they should visit."

Sloan sighs. "Fine. I decided to take this class because I needed some CEUs. I didn't want to lose my license so here I am." He holds up his hands covered in salt. "And yes, I knew instructor Soggs. He and I went to massage school together. We're friends online and when I saw his post about the class I signed up. Now are there any more questions, Mrs. Parker because I would like to go wash my hands?"

I shake my head as he stomps over to the sink.

"Wow, he's touchy," Olive mumbles then puts the lid on her salt scrub. "And I found this class on a massage website."

"Mr. Gillman said you were in the kitchen with Instructor Soggs before he fell. Did he seem upset about anything?"

Olive blows a strand of hair from her face then says, "Um, no. Not really. We were just talking about our businesses then he excused himself to go upstairs. I finished making my sandwich then the next thing I know he was crashing down the stairs." She bursts into tears and rushes toward the bathroom.

I sigh and wipe my hands on the towel next to me.

"Making friends?"

I jump and turn to find Travis standing behind me. "What are you doing here?"

"I have some questions for your fellow classmates as well."

"Good luck," I mumble then begin cleaning up the table.

"Why? Are you not having any?" He asks, helping me pack up supplies.

I glance over at Sloan, who's whispering in Paula's ear and they're both glaring over at me. I'm putting them at the top of my suspect list. I lower my voice and say, "I 'saw' Sloan fighting with the Instructor at the top of the stairs when our hands touched reaching for the same oil. Sloan said he went to school with the instructor, maybe there's some bad blood there." I chew on my lip and try not to look at Paula, even though I can feel her eyes on me. "Paula wasn't wearing her scrubs last night, maybe because she snagged them on the nail by the stairs. Did you get the sample results back yet?"

"Not yet. The lab's backed up, but hopefully later today." Travis says, handing me the jars of salt scrubs then taking in my somber expression. "Hey, at least you got some information, right?"

"Yeah, but at what cost?"

He frowns. "What do you mean?"

I subtly nod toward Sloan. "I think he's warning the others that I'm asking questions about their connection to the instructor."

"Hmm. I wouldn't let that deter you." He pauses then asks, "Did you see anything else in your vision?"

I open my mouth to tell him no when Paula comes over to the table.

"Detective Mills, what are you doing here?" She runs a nail down his arm and steps closer to him.

Travis shoots me a pleading look, but I simply shrug to let him know he's on his own. "I came to ask you and your classmates some questions about Instructor Soggs."

"Oh, really. I figured that was Autumn's job." She gives me a fake smile. "I mean it sounds like she's already interrogating everyone, why I have no idea, since the instructor's fall was an accident."

Travis clears his throat and speaks loudly so everyone can hear him. "No, Instructor Soggs was murdered."

5
———

"**M**urdered?! Is this a joke? I thought he fell down the stairs," Anita inquires, joining our conversation. Her blond hair is pulled up into a high bun a top her head and her face is free of make-up except for her bright red lipstick.

"Yeah, that's what Olive said." George states, stepping up next to his wife. They are the 'perfect couple' with their matching black scrubs and blond hair with green eyes.

"Olive's still in the bathroom, but that's pretty much what she told me." I offer, hoping it will keep the group from getting defensive and completely shutting down.

Travis gives me a perplexed look before addressing the group. "We suspect Mr. Soggs was pushed down the stairs."

Anita gasps. "No. How do you know?"

"There's evidence of a struggle at the top of the stairs." Travis gives me a look, one I'll have to ask him about later.

"So, someone in this room killed Instructor Soggs?" Anita's eyes are wide as she glances around the room.

"It would seem so unless Mr. Gillman has a ghost or a guest we didn't account for last night."

"Well I've heard all about the crime in this little town of yours," George says, crossing his arms over his chest. "It wouldn't surprise me if someone snuck in and pushed the instructor down the stairs."

Travis furrows his brow. "Why would someone do that?"

George throws up his hands. "Who knows! This town has been in the news almost every month it seems." He turns to his wife. "I told you coming here was a bad idea. Now, there's a killer on the loose and we're staying in that death trap another night. I think we should cut our losses and leave."

"No one's going anywhere. This is an active investigation and all of you are suspects," Travis declares, glaring at George before taking out his tablet and typing in a few things.

"What are you writing?" George demands, trying to peek at Travis's screen.

Travis presses the device against his chest. "It's official police business. I would like to question each of you... alone." He glances back and forth between George and Anita.

"We have nothing to hide." George puffs out his chest and wraps an arm around his wife's shoulder. "Right, sweetheart?"

Anita nods slowly, but appears to be in shock... or is it something else?

I turn to find Sloan trying to slip out down the hallway. "I think you should question Sloan, first, Detective," I say, loudly so there's no way Sloan can't hear me.

Everyone turns to stare at Sloan, who freezes at the sound of his name.

He glares at me then straightens and stomps over to Travis.

"Where were you off to Mr. Burke?" Travis gestures to the office where Paula's leaning against the door frame.

"I was going to get some more essential oil bottles," Sloan states, not meeting Travis's eyes.

"We have plenty here," Regina pipes up then gestures with her hand to showcase the array of bottles on the table.

Sloan turns red and storms into the office, bumping Paula's shoulder and causing her to stagger back into the office.

"Hey, what was that for?" Paula demands, pushing against Sloan's chest.

Sloan rolls his eyes and flops down in one of the office chairs.

"If you'll please excuse us, Miss Arnold. I'll be with you once I'm finished talking with Mr. Burke."

"Anything for you, Detective," Paula coos, running a hand down Travis's striped tie.

Travis clears his throat and steps back, causing Paula to lose her balance. He reaches out to catch her and she takes the opportunity to wrap her arms around his neck and press her lips to his.

I don't know what comes over me, but one second I'm completely calm and the next I'm lunging at Paula. I dig my fingers into her arms and yank her out of Travis's grasp.

"Hey!" Paula objects, shaking me off and rubbing her arm where my fingerprints left red blotches.

I ball my fists and start toward her when Olive comes out of the bathroom.

"What's going on?" Olive cries, moving toward the break room as to not get in the way of my attack.

Arms wrap around my waist and Travis pulls me into the bathroom and shuts the door.

"What are you doing?" I cry, struggling against him to try and get to the door.

"Aut, breathe."

"I am breathing, otherwise I wouldn't be about ready to slap Paula silly for kissing you. Can't you arrest her for harassment or something?" I huff, blowing a strand of hair out of my face.

Travis smirks at me. "Harassment?"

"You didn't want her to kiss you..." I pause then ask quietly, "Or did you?" I stare at his tie. The tie Paula was running her hand down only moments ago. The thought of looking into his green eyes and seeing that he liked her kiss is almost too much to bear. Why, I have no idea?

"Aut, look at me."

I shake my head, tears pooling in my eyes because I shouldn't be feeling these feelings. I love Josh. Miss him terribly and I'm not ready to move on. It's only been seven months. My heart can't love Travis or feel anything for Travis. I've buried those feelings. I thought they were gone... but I guess they're not.

"Autumn," Travis lowers his voice and tugs at my chin so I'm forced to look him in the eye.

I blink back the tears, but one escapes and he wipes it away with his thumb.

"What's going on? Why are you so upset?"

Before I can answer him, Regina's knocking on the door. "Open up. I have a restless crew out here and I need reinforcements. Oh and Mr. Burke left out the front door before I could stop him."

Travis looks torn on what to do.

"Go."

"Aut..."

"Go, we can talk later."

He squeezes my hand then bursts through the door and takes off down the hallway, leaving me to figure out my feelings.

I let out the breath I've been holding and straighten my shoulders.

Regina quirks a perfectly plucked eyebrow at me. "Care to share what just happened?"

"Not really."

She nods with a smirk. "Splash some water on your face then join us in the massage room. We'll get this class back on track."

I do as she says and pat my face dry with a towel. When I look in the mirror, Josh is standing over my shoulder with a smile on his face. I turn to throw my arms around him but when I do, he's gone. I blink then rub my eyes. Did I imagine him? "Please come back," I whisper.

"Autumn, who are you talking to?" Cat pokes her head in and looks around the bathroom.

"No one. Just trying to get myself together."

"I was next door taking some salt scrubs to Allison when we saw Mr. Burke running out of the spa." Then she pauses and lowers her voice, "Aunt Regina said you nearly ripped off Paula's head when she kissed dad. Is that true?"

"Ripped off her head is a bit of an exaggeration. I nearly pulled her away from your dad. He's a detective and she's a suspect. It's not professional of her to act that way toward an officer of the law."

Cat cocks her head to the side with a smirk on her face. "Are you sure that's all it was?"

"Of course, what else would it be?" I step out of the bathroom and into the break room to make myself some tea. My hands are still shaking from seeing Josh... *did I see him or did I imagine him?* My heart's racing ninety to nothing in my chest. *Was he there because he's upset I got so worked up over Travis and Paula? He was smiling so maybe he was happy... or maybe...*

"Autumn? Where'd you go?"

"Hmm?" I take a cup out of the cabinet and nearly drop it when I see Josh appear behind Cat.

"Autumn, are you ok? Do I need to take you to see a doctor? You're really pale." Cat steps up to me and takes the cup out of my hand then places a hand on my forehead. "Are you feeling sick? Maybe you should lie down on the couch."

I'm still staring at my dead husband's ghost. He's smiling again then winks at me before he disappears. My heart's thumping so loudly in my chest, I feel like it might explode. *Why is Josh here?* I've been wanting to see him for months. Hoping he would come and visit me like Laura did, but he never did. *Why is he showing up now? Does he think I'm going to move on and forget him?* I sway slightly and reach out to steady myself on the counter.

"Autumn, you need to sit down. You're as white as a ghost." Cat leads me over to the couch then hurries over to the stove to make me some tea.

I swallow the lump in my throat then realize why Josh is here. This was the weekend I was going to scatter his ashes by our tree in the woods. He must be stuck here until I do. I brought his ashes to work this weekend so he would "be here in spirit" for the class. It sounds morbid, I know, but I just felt like I needed to bring them. Now, his spirit is actually here and I'm not sure what he wants. I need to talk to him, but he's not going to talk to me with Cat around. Not to mention, I can't leave Regina to teach a room full of potential murder suspects.

"Here, drink this," Cat orders, handing me a cup of tea

then sitting down next me. "You look like you're a million miles away. What are you thinking about? You and dad?"

I hate to disappoint her, but I'm not going to lie to her either. I take a sip of tea then say, "Actually, I was thinking about Josh."

Cat's shoulders slump, but then her face turns sympathetic. "It must be hard being here without him, huh?"

I nod. "Although I feel like he's here in spirit."

She pats my leg. "I'm sure he is."

"Autumn? What are you doing in here? I know you need those CEUs to keep your license active. I can't sign off on it if you don't actually attend the classes," Regina says, with her hands on her hips.

"Aunt Regina, Autumn's not feeling well. I think she needs to rest."

"Oh, dear. What's wrong?" Regina comes over and feels my forehead. "You don't feel hot. Is it your stomach?"

I shake my head. "More like my heart."

"Ah," she nods her head in understanding. "This has to do with what happened a few minutes ago and you feeling like you're betraying Josh, doesn't it?"

I shrug, not sure how to answer.

She studies me for a moment. "Or is it being here at this class he booked for the two of you without him?"

I shrug again because I don't want to tell them Josh's ghost is haunting me. *Is he even haunting me?* I'm not sure.

"Well I think the best thing to do is finish this class. It will keep your mind off things and give you an opportunity to ask some questions. I put you with the newlyweds since I was afraid you might strangle Paula," Regina jokes, holding out a hand to help me to my feet.

I laugh and hand Cat my cup before taking Regina's hand. "I wouldn't strangle her."

She quirks an eyebrow at me. "Oh, really. So, what were you planning to do before Travis yanked you into the bathroom? For which, I plan to get details about later."

"Nothing happened in the bathroom. He was trying to calm me down. I honestly don't know what came over me. It was like some kind of switch flipped and just seeing Paula kiss Travis made me want to rip off her lips and shove them down her throat."

Cat giggles. "It sounds like you were jealous."

"Jealous? Me? No." I frown and think about how I felt. Those feelings felt an awful lot like jealousy, but how could I be jealous? Travis and I aren't even dating. We haven't been a couple in years. I saw him kiss Allison without a hint of jealousy so why now? What's changed?

"We'll let you think about that for a little while, dear. Now, let's get back in there before the rest of the class decides to up and leave like Mr. Burke." She tugs me down the hall and toward the massage room. When we pass the receptionist area, I see Josh standing by the window. He's looking at something then turns to me and smiles before pointing at one of the pictures on the wall.

"I'll be right there, Regina. I just need to check on something up front."

"Alright, dear, but please hurry. We've wasted a lot of time already."

I step into the waiting room and slowly toward Josh's ghost. He watches me with his blue eyes. When I reach the window, he disappears. I open my mouth to call out to him, but decide to look at what he was pointing at instead. A picture is tucked where he was pointing. It's a picture of Paula and Instructor Soggs. He has his arm wrapped her as she beams up at him. I smile and grab the photo then whisper, "Thank you."

6

I step into the room and search for Paula. She's sitting on the massage table swinging her legs back and forth. Everyone else is surrounding Regina and seems enthralled in what she's showing them. I hop up on the table next to Paula. "Not interested in this portion?"

She shrugs and continues to stare down at the floor.

"I'm sorry about a little bit ago. I don't know what came over me."

She smirks. "It's pretty obvious."

I frown. "What is?"

"You're in love with the detective."

I scoff. "I am not. I'm married."

"Were married. Your husband's dead."

I cringe at her words.

"Sorry. I don't mean to be insensitive. It's just pretty clear that you have feelings for the hot detective."

I ignore the churning in my gut and the one in my heart and focus on the case. I slip the photo out of my scrub pocket and hold it out to her. "I didn't realize you and Instructor Soggs were so close."

Paula snatches the photo out of my hand and presses it to her chest. "Where did you get his?"

Now it's my turn to shrug. "Why does it matter? You look awful smitten with the instructor."

She snorts and glances down at the picture. "I was."

"But he wasn't?"

A tear falls down her cheek and she brushes it off. "No. Yes. I don't know. One minute he's hopelessly in love with me and then the next he's breaking up with me."

"And that made you angry."

She glares at me. "Of course, it made me angry. He acted like he loved me then threw me aside like I was yesterday's trash. All because of her."

"Her?"

Paula stares at the photo, but doesn't answer.

"Autumn, can I see you for a minute?" Travis calls from the doorway. His cheeks are red from chasing Sloan, sweat's dripping from his brow and his red hair's standing up in all directions.

I glance at Paula, who's still staring at the photo then hop off the table and head over to Travis.

Regina shoots me a smirk then returns her attention to the other students.

"I'll be lucky if she gives me any credits for this class," I mumble to Travis.

He winks at his aunt. "I'm sure she'll let you make up the hours somehow."

I nod and sigh then ask, "What's up? Did you find Sloan?"

Travis shakes his head then runs a hand through his hair. "No, I have several guys out looking for him. It's starting to rain so I don't think he'll get too far. He rode to the spa with Paula and her car's still in the parking lot."

"I'm sure we'll find him."

He furrows his brow then studies me for a moment. "Did you and Paula make-up?" Travis gestures toward her.

Tears are running down her cheeks as she continues to stare at the photo.

"Why is she crying?"

I glance over my shoulder at her. "It turns out Paula and the instructor had a fling or a relationship. I think it was more of a relationship to her and a fling to him." I don't mention where the picture came from.

"Huh, he's kind of old for her."

I smack his arm. "Love has no age limit."

He smirks at me then shakes his head. "There's my Aut and her hopeless romantic notions." Then his smirk turns into a frown. "I mean... not my Aut... it's just you haven't been yourself lately and I miss you... I mean..." He rakes a hand through his hair again.

I cut him off. "It's fine, Travis. I know I haven't been myself. It's been hard losing Josh. Not just because he was my husband, but because he was the person I told every-thing to. I have Nikki, but she's busy getting ready for the babies and running her yoga studio."

"You have me," Travis whispers.

I shoot him a smile. "I know. I just don't know what we are right now so it's hard to talk to you."

He takes my hand and pulls me down the hall into an empty massage room. Then gestures to the massage table. We both hop up on it and stare at the ground in silence before Travis says, "Autumn, I meant what I said to you last night in the car. I'm not in a hurry. If being your friend is what you need, then I'm here. You can talk about Josh. Cry. Get angry. I'll even watch those rom-com-'s you love so much. Whatever you need, I'm here." He turns and takes my hand in his. "Please don't shut me out. I want to be here for you."

I squeeze his hand and swallow the lump in my throat. "I know. Thank you. I'll try to be more open and get back to myself. It's just hard."

Travis squeezes my hand back. "I know it is and that's why you need to let us help you. Me, Cat, Regina, pretty much the whole town would do anything for you. You just have to tell us what you need and then consider it done."

I smile and nod at him as tears stream down my face.

He brushes them away with his thumb then tips my chin up so I look him in the eye. "What can I do?"

"Solve this case."

He grins. "That I can do, but only with your help." He drops his hand and crosses them over his chest. "How do you know Paula and the instructor were dating? And where did that photo come from? Did she have it in her scrubs?"

I shake my head and chew on my lip. I'm not sure if I should tell Travis that Josh was here or... is here. *Will he even believe me or think I'm imagining things?*

"Aut? What's wrong? You have that look on your face like you want to tell me something, but you know I'm not going to like it."

I roll my eyes.

"What?" Travis shrugs then narrows his eyes at me. "I know you. Now, tell me what you don't want to tell me. I can handle it."

I chew on my lip and contemplate my options which aren't many.

He sighs. "Autumn, just tell me."

I take a deep breath and just decide to blurt it out. "Josh came to see me while you were chasing Sloan. I found the picture in the waiting room because I think he put it there for me."

Travis blinks then blinks again. "Josh is here? Like right now?"

I glance around the room then shake my head.

"Was he angry? Does he not want me here?"

"No, he was smiling. It's more like he wants to help me... us solve this case."

Travis frowns. "Why?"

I shrug. "I brought his ashes here so he could be with me this weekend before I spread them by our tree. Maybe that's why he's here."

Travis doesn't say anything just stares at the wall like he's really thinking about something.

I decide to add another theory. "Maybe since Josh's case isn't solved, he's planning to stick around until it is and help me with this case in the meantime."

"So, he's here because we haven't found his killer?"

I shrug again like the fact that my dead husband is here isn't a big deal. "Laura stayed here at the spa until we found her killer. Josh is probably doing the same thing."

"Or..."

"Or what?"

"Or he didn't really mean what he wrote in that letter and he's here to make sure you don't fall in love with me... again." Travis scans the room like he's waiting for Josh to appear and confirm his accusation.

"That's ridiculous."

"Is it? This will be the first case me and you can solve just the two of us. A chance for us to really work together."

"We've always worked together on cases."

"But Josh was always there for you to bounce theories off

of and to work on coming up with suspects. Maybe he's not ready to let you go. That's why he left the photo for you."

I furrow my brow and open my mouth to say something when Josh appears behind Travis and he doesn't look happy.

"What? What's wrong?" Travis asks, taking in my shocked expression.

I point behind him and he turns around slowly.

"Josh," he croaks.

Josh just frowns at him and shakes his head then disappears.

Travis doesn't move for what seems like hours, but it's really only a few minutes. When he finally turns back around to face me, he says, "I take it I'm wrong about that?"

"I think so. I'm going to go with my theory that he's waiting for his killer to be caught so he can move on."

Travis jumps down off the table and holds out a hand to help me down. "Well I guess that's my cue to head back to the station and dig into his case." He gestures for me to lead the way.

"I'll see what I can find out about Paula and the instructor's relationship. She said something about another woman getting in between them. Was the instructor married?"

"Not that I know of. His next of kin was his mother so I would assume not."

My eyes widen. "Maybe she was the one who got in between her son and Paula's relationship."

"I'll have to check his file again. I called her last night to inform her of her son's death. She was pretty devastated. He was her only child and it seemed like they were close. She'll be in town later today. I'll be sure to set up a time for you to meet her. Maybe you'll get a vision when you shake her hand or something."

I nod. "That sounds good. Well I'd better get back to class or your aunt's going to fail me."

He chuckles. "I doubt it. She's a stickler for the rules, but she also knows we're trying to catch a killer."

"True." I bite my lip, my mind racing with different scenarios. "I'll see what I can find out. Dinner at the café? Say, 5:30?"

Travis smiles slyly. "Why Autumn are you asking me out on a date?"

I feel my cheeks warm then smack his arm. "No. No. It's to share information. That's it. It's not a date." I chew on my lip to stop my rambling when I see Travis's face fall slightly. I take a deep breath and square my shoulders to regain control of the situation especially since I'm feeling completely out of control. "It's an information gathering session. Plus, I expect you to bring a date."

Travis's eyes bulge and his jaw drops. "A d-date? W-what? Why? Who?"

Now, it's my turn to give him a sly smile. "The instructor's mother, of course."

7

———

"Autumn, over here," Travis calls from the corner booth of the café.

I wave to a few members from the Crafty Crew as I make my way over to him. Some of the members wink at me then whisper amongst themselves. I can only imagine what they're saying not to mention what the gossip will be around town in the next fifteen minutes. Probably something crazy like Travis and I eloped. Ugh. This town and their endless need to talk about everyone and everything and it's only gotten worse. Last month, Travis took a couple days off to spend some time with Cat and rumors flew that we were finally dating. It took two weeks for him to squash them. I didn't comment on it because what's the point? Travis knew it upset me so he put the kibosh on things. I have to admit having Travis look out for me was pretty sweet. Although he's always been protective and considerate when it comes to me... well anyone really. He's a good guy. I sigh and push those thoughts away as I approach the table.

I square my shoulders and take a deep breath to try and

get myself out of this funk before I meet the instructor's mother. I'm feeling pretty glum after spending the afternoon treated like I had a contagious disease or something. They stayed as far away from me as possible. No one would even look my way let alone talk to me. Regina kept us busy until it was almost time to go. Paula shut down completely and barely said two words before shooting out the door as soon as Regina dismissed the class. Everyone else left quickly too. I sigh and force a smile as I reach Travis's table.

There's an older lady probably in her late sixties sitting across from him. Her gray hair is cut short and curled tightly on her head. She's wearing a long black dress with a matching colored designer bag. Her wrinkled face is pale with dark circles under her blue eyes. I nod to Travis and keep my greeting formal because this isn't a date... it's business, "Hello, Detective Mills."

"Mrs. Parker," he raises an eyebrow at me, but thankfully doesn't question my formality. "This is Mrs. Soggs. She just got into town. Mrs. Soggs, this is Autumn Parker. She owns the spa where your son was teaching a class this weekend."

"It's nice to meet you, Mrs. Soggs," I say, shaking her hand then slipping into the booth next to Travis.

Mrs. Soggs sniffles and wipes her nose with her handkerchief. "You too, dear. Oh, Tony was so upset that the classes kept getting cancelled due to the snow and his busy schedule. I tried to convince him to just cancel it indefinitely, but he was adamant about having it." She sighs and looks out the window. Tears form in her eyes and she dabs a handkerchief at the corners. "I think Tony wanted to come here because of his dad."

"His dad?" I cock my head in confusion.

Mrs. Soggs smiles sadly. "Yes, Tony Senior and I used to

stay at the little bed and breakfast down the road every year for our anniversary. I would come home and talk about the place. It was so quaint and charming. Tony Jr. always loved listening to my stories and said one day he planned to visit. I guess that's why he wanted to come here so badly." She sniffles. "Now, he's gone and you're saying he was m-murdered," she wails into her hands.

Travis shifts uneasily in his seat and shoots me a pleading look.

I reach out and pat Mrs. Soggs's hand. "We're so sorry for your loss." I pause and give her a minute to collect herself. "We're hoping you can help us find his killer."

She dabs her eyes again and straightens her shoulders. "Of course. Anything. Although I'm not sure there's much I can tell you. My Tony was a private man. When he moved out of the house last year and in with his fiancée, we kind of lost touch."

"Fiancée?" I exchange a curious glance with Travis.

"Yes. They met at a class he was teaching. I personally thought it was unprofessional of him to date a student, but I guess they went to school together." She sighs and rolls her eyes. "He was in love."

"So, you didn't have a good relationship with his fiancée?"

Mrs. Soggs shrugs. "It wasn't that we didn't have a good relationship. It was just... well she was hard to get to know. Kind of different."

I smirk, thinking of Paula with her rose colored hair and tattoos. "She definitely is."

"Oh, you know her?"

I nod. "She's part of the class this weekend although she didn't mention that she was engaged to Tony."

Mrs. Soggs sighs again. "They broke up a few months

back. I'm surprised she's even here. The break-up wasn't pretty."

I frown. "Do you mind if I ask what happened?"

"The only thing Tony would tell me is that she found someone else." Mrs. Soggs dabs her eyes. "She broke his heart. When he would come by or talk to me on the phone, he wasn't himself. He was moping around and working a bunch. That girl really did a number on him."

I chew on my lower lip contemplating my interaction with Paula at the spa. She seemed devastated by the break-up and even told me it was Tony who broke up with her. I open my mouth to ask my next question when Paula walks into the diner.

She scans the room then her gaze falls on me. Her eyes narrow as she stomps toward me and slams her hand down on the table, causing us all to jump.

"Hello, Paula," I greet, cutting her off from making a spectacle in front of Tony's mother. "You remember Mrs. Soggs, don't you?"

Paula's eyes widen and she turns slightly to assess Mrs. Soggs. "It's a pleasure to meet you," her tone turning softer and her eyes filling with tears.

Travis and I exchange a confused glance.

"You mean you two have never met?"

Paula sticks out her hand and ignores my question. "Tony talked a lot about you."

Mrs. Soggs gives her a sad smile and takes her hand. "I take it you were a friend of my Tony's."

"Yes, I'm Paula."

"Please sit. Join us," Mrs. Soggs scoots over so Paula can sit down next to her.

My head starts to throb because this doesn't make any sense. "I'm sorry. I'm confused."

Both women turn their attention to me, but it's Paula who asks, "About what?"

"I thought you told me that you and Tony dated."

"We did."

"But you never met his mother?"

Paula shakes her head. "He was planning to introduce us at Christmas, but then he broke up with me out of nowhere."

Mrs. Soggs frowns. "You were dating my Tony? But he was engaged to be married."

Paula's eyes widen. "Engaged? He told me they were just dating. When I saw them together, he told me he was confused and trying to sort out his feelings. He asked for some space so we broke up."

"Oh, dear." Mrs. Soggs turns pale. "Tony proposed over a year ago. They were planning to get married this weekend."

Tears fill Paula's eyes then she jumps up and dashes out the door without a word to anyone.

"Oh, my. I didn't mean to upset the poor thing. Tony never even mentioned her."

My head's really starting to pound so I rub my temples.

"Are you okay, Autumn?" Travis whispers and reaches out to rub my back. "You're probably hungry, aren't you?" He raises his hand to signal the waitress, a teenager with a blond ponytail bounces over to the table and he orders me a soup and salad then gestures to Mrs. Soggs to order some food.

"Oh, I'll have what she's having, dear," Mrs. Soggs tells the waitress.

My stomach growls at the mention of food so I take a sip of water and try to focus back on Mrs. Soggs, who is folding up her menu and handing it to the waitress. I straighten my shoulders and will my headache away before asking, "If Paula wasn't Tony's fiancée then who was?"

"You don't know? I thought you said she was taking the class this weekend."

"Well I thought his fiancée was Paula. Since that's not the case then I don't know who it is... or was," I reply, softly.

"Her name was Ana. She was a pretty little thing. Not quite my Tony's type. I would say Paula was more his type, but he was over the moon in love with Miss Ana." Mrs. Soggs rolls her eyes again. "I didn't like her, but I wish it would have worked out for them. At least then he would have been happy before he died." She sniffles and shakes her head as our food arrives.

I dig into my soup and contemplate the situation. I can feel Travis's eyes on me as I eat. I reach out to grab the pepper at the same time Mrs. Soggs does and a vision hits me like a lightning bolt. It comes so fast, it takes my breath away.

Mrs. Soggs and Tony are in a heated discussion. Tony accuses her of cutting him out of the family business and threatens to go to the police.

"Let go," Mrs. Soggs whisper yells, jerking her hand away from me. It's then that I realize I was squeezing it tightly.

My face heats up as I drop my hands into my lap and mutter an apology.

She eyes me suspiciously then turns back to her dinner.

I take a few bites of my salad so I have some time to process what I saw. Did Mrs. Soggs have something to do with her son's death? Tony threatening to turn her in for something is a strong motive for murder, but he was her son, would he really do that to his own mother? Would she really kill him? Plus, she wasn't at the inn, or was she? She did say she and her husband used to stay there. Did she know Mr. Gillman? Were they friends? Could he have helped her... commit murder? And what is she doing that's illegal? I have so many questions racing through my mind. The room starts to spin. I take a deep breath to try and calm my nerves and focus on questioning Mrs. Soggs when the lights go out.

8

———

"Autumn! Autumn! Can you hear me?"

I blink and look around, it's then that I realize I'm lying on the floor. The lights are blaring overheard and I raise my hand to block them. "I'm fine. The lights went out. What happened?"

Travis frowns and helps me sit up. "Autumn, the lights didn't go out, you passed out."

My eyes grow wide. "What?"

He nods. "I've called the ambulance. They're on their way."

I blink again and try to remember feeling faint or weak, but nothing comes to mind. I remember thinking about the case and my head was really throbbing, but otherwise I was just hungry. "I'm perfectly fine. No need to worry. Maybe I should head home and lie down."

"No, you're going to the hospital," Travis states as he lifts me into his arm and heads toward the door.

"Travis, put me down," I demand, trying to squirm out of his arms, but it doesn't do any good. The man's built like a machine and the more I move the tighter his grip. I spot

Mrs. Soggs slipping out the side door without paying. I open my mouth to call out to her when a blast of hot air hits me and takes my breath away. The sun's setting, but the humidity is in full force. It's sticky and the air's gotten heavier since I went into the café. It must be getting ready to rain. "Travis, the bill. We didn't pay and Mrs. Soggs just took off out the side door."

"I told the waitress to put it on my tab. I'll pay them tomorrow. Now, stop squirming."

Sirens and lights come blaring into the parking lot and Taylor jumps out with another EMT.

"I thought she was unconscious," Taylor demands, putting her hands on her hips and glaring at me.

"She came to while we were waiting on you, but she's refusing to go to the hospital. She's going whether she wants to or not."

"You can't make me go, Travis. I was probably just light-headed from not eating. I skipped lunch. You know how I get when my blood sugar drops."

"You were eating when you fainted," he argues then sets me down inside the ambulance and bends down to look me in the eyes. "Please let the doctor check you out. Cat says you've been getting more headaches lately. She's worried about you."

"I'm fine."

"You might be and I pray you are, but please go to the hospital. If not for me, for Cat."

I huff and cross my arms because when he pulls the Cat card, I can't refuse. "Fine." I let Taylor check my blood pressure and try not to wince when she pumps the cuff a little tighter than she needs to. I know she's mad that she and Travis didn't work out, but don't take it out on me. Although she probably sees it as my fault since Travis has made it clear of his intentions when it comes to me. I sigh and rest my head back on the stretcher as we make our way to the hospital.

Travis hasn't let go of my hand and I can feel his eyes on me. I know he's worried and if I'm being honest, I kind of am too. My headaches have gotten more intense over the past few months. Really ever since my visions started. Did Lindy ever have these kinds of headaches? If she did then I can see why she didn't like her 'gift'.

When we reach the hospital, I'm taken directly to get an MRI and then a CT before I'm finally wheeled into a room where they draw a ton of blood. My stomach turns at the sight of all the vials then I'm left alone, but only for a minute.

"Autumn, how are you feeling?" Travis asks softly, stepping into the room.

"Tired," I sigh, closing my eyes. "You should be at the station or home with Cat. I'm just going to sleep here for the night." I yawn.

"Yeah, we both know that's not going to happen. Besides, Cat and Regina are hanging out at the inn to make sure no one leaves."

My eyes fly open. "What?! By themselves? One of those strangers could be the killer. You can't let them stay there. What is wrong with you?" I throw the covers off my legs while the heart monitor's going crazy next me.

A young brunette nurse comes rushing in. "What's going on in here?" She demands. "What are you doing out of bed? You should be resting."

"Yes, Autumn. Please calm down. They're fine. I have three officers at the inn with them. They're safe."

I take a deep breath and try to calm my racing heart. I feel light headed and sit down on the bed. The nurse helps me lie back and covers me up before shooting Travis a stern look.

"No more upsetting Mrs. Parker, do you hear me, Captain? She needs to rest." Then she mutters something about him upsetting all the women in town.

His face grows red and he rakes a hand through his hair.

"What was that about?"

"Taylor's been very vocal about her displeasure in me 'leading' her on."

I frown. "Did you?"

He shrugs. "Regina was pushing for me to get out and date more after you and Josh got married. She set up the dinner with Taylor. I showed up because it would have been rude not to plus Lindy gave me a part in the dinner theater. It's not like I could have bailed on that."

"True. You would have been the victim instead of Lindy. She was scary when you didn't go along with her plans." I shiver at the thought of Lindy's wrath even though I know she's six feet under and there's no way she can hurt me.

Travis sits down in the chair next to my bed and rests his arms on his knees. "Autumn, is something going on?"

"What do you mean?"

"The headaches. The fainting. This isn't the first time. You seem to always end up in the hospital when we're on a case."

"Hey, that's not fair. It's not always because I faint. One time I was poisoned. Another time I fell trying to take down an alleged perp."

He sighs. "I know, but the headaches are getting worse, aren't they? You had headaches in high school, but these seem to be something else. Something bigger. More serious. Do you think they have to do with your visions? Are they playing a role in your health?"

"Maybe," I whisper. "They have gotten worse since I've been getting more visions."

Travis growls. "That's it, no more. I shouldn't have asked you to try and see what happened to the instructor." He rakes another hand through his hair. "This is all my fault."

"It's not your fault and I can't control my visions. They just come to me." I pause and chew on my lip for a moment before I say, "I did see Mrs. Soggs and Tony fighting when I touched her hand at the café."

He eyes grow wide. "You did? What were they fighting about?"

"Tony was accusing of cutting him out of the family business. He was threatening to turn her into the police."

Travis frowns. "I'll look into it."

I nibble on my lower lip for a minute then ask, "Do you think Mrs. Soggs killed her son?"

Travis's eyes grow wide. "What? No. Why would you even think that? She's heartbroken not to mention she wasn't even in town yesterday."

"Remember how Mrs. Soggs said that she and her husband used to say at an inn every year for their anniversary. She had to have known Mr. Gillman. Could he have hidden her or worse... killed Tony?"

"Mr. Gillman said he was downstairs in the den when the instructor fell."

"No one was around to verify his story though. He said that the Cases's had gone to bed, Paula and Sloan were in their rooms and Olive was in the kitchen. Mr. Gillman could have pushed the instructor or worse, the instructor's mother could have pushed him and Mr. Gillman's hiding her in one of the other rooms."

"What other room, Autumn? The inn's booked with

everyone from the class. There are only five rooms and one of those is Mr. Gillman's."

I open my mouth to tell him my next theory when he cuts me off.

"No, Autumn. Mr. Gillman wasn't hiding Mrs. Soggs in his room. They aren't having some secret love affair and going to run off together."

"How do you know?" I cross my arms over my chest and stick out my chin in a pout.

He rolls his eyes. "It's a solid theory. I'll look into it, but in the mean time you need to rest. No more visions. You need to take it easy."

"I agree with the Captain," a familiar voice says from the doorway.

"Dr. Gregory? What are you doing here?" I ask, smiling at him.

Dr. Gregory steps into the room, nodding to each of us. "Autumn. Captain Mills. It's good to see you both."

Travis stands and moves out of his way so he can assess me. "It's nice to see you as well, doc. What are you doing back in town?"

"I'm leading some training classes for smaller hospitals in the surrounding areas. This week I'm here in Daysville. I'd planned to call you and see if we could all meet at Pete's to catch up, but it's been rather busy around here." He glances down at his iPad then back up at me with sympathetic eyes. "Autumn, I was sorry to hear about Josh. He was a good man."

Tears blur my eyes and I blink them back. "Thank you," I squeak out.

Travis gives me a sad look too, which almost makes me lose it, but I take a deep breath and get my emotions in check.

Dr. Gregory clears his throat. "I couldn't help over-hearing what the Captain said about taking it easy and not seeing any visions. Is this a new thing?"

I nod. "They started about a year ago. I can see flashes of people's lives and either get a headache before or after them... sometimes both."

"Hmm. So, your headaches have gotten worse and now, you're fainting too?"

"I guess so." I wince because I have a bad feeling about what he's going to say.

Dr. Gregory's quiet for a moment then says quietly, "Autumn, we found a mass on your brain."

My heart stops beating for a minute and my lunges seize up in my chest before Travis grabs my hand. I blink, feeling like I'm having an out of body experience. Maybe I'm dreaming. I pinch myself to wake-up, but I realize quickly, I'm living this nightmare

"It's going to be okay, Autumn. You're going to be okay," Travis says, trying to reassure me.

Dr. Gregory continues, "You have a tumor. It's small. We can remove it, but we need to do so immediately. I can put you on my schedule for Monday."

"Monday? Like in two days?" I choke out.

"The sooner the better. We need to determine if it's cancerous and if so move forward with treatment."

Tears well up in my eyes and the room blurs.

Travis squeezes my hand tighter. "You're going to be fine, Autumn."

"If you're ok with it, I'll go ahead and schedule the surgery."

I nod because I don't know what else to do. I'm completely numb.

Dr. Gregory squeezes my arm. "You should get some rest," he orders before leaving.

I try to breathe. Try to think. Try to process, but my mind's blank. I should be thinking about my options. Do I really want surgery? Chemo? Bile rises in my throat and I choke it back.

Travis strokes the top of my hand. "Autumn, talk to me."

I look down at our hands. "What if I die?"

Travis stiffens, not expecting those words. "You're not going to die. Dr. Gregory said the tumor or mass or whatever it is, is small. He'll remove it and you'll be fine." He pauses and blinks several times before whispering, "You have to be." He brings my hand to his lips. His breath is warm against my skin and I savor it. His phone beeps, but he ignores it. Then it begins to ring.

"You should get that."

"It's not important," he closes his eyes and places his forehead on our hands. "Nothing matters except getting you better." A tear falls from his eye, but he doesn't bother to wipe it away. "You're going to be fine," he repeats and I'm not sure if he's trying to convince me or himself.

I reach out and run my fingers through his hair. It's been a long time since I've done that and it's like finding your old favorite sweatshirt. It's familiar and comforting.

Travis's phone goes off again, but he doesn't let go of my hands.

"Travis, you can get the phone. Life has to go on. We have a case to solve."

He shakes his head. "No."

"No?" I raise an eyebrow at him.

"No, there are officers for that. You need to rest and I don't plan to leave your side."

I frown although his words touch my heart this isn't

what I want. If I die on Monday, I want to have this case closed. I have to know who killed the instructor and if this tumor is giving me the ability to have visions then I need to use it to solve this case. "Travis, we have to solve this case. I need to solve this case before I have surgery."

"Autumn, no. You need to rest. The last time you had a vision, you passed out. You can't risk it. It's too dangerous."

"I won't push myself, I promise."

Travis's phone rings again and he growls.

"Please get it, it could be about the case."

He sighs and takes his phone from his pocket. "Mills," he barks into the phone.

I watch him as he listens to whatever the person on the other end is telling him. When he hangs up, he has a stern look on his face.

"What? What's wrong?"

"They found Sloan."

"They did? Where? Why did he run? Is he talking?"

Travis shakes his head.

"No? He's not talking? Why not?"

"Because he's dead."

9

"**D**ead?"

Travis sets his phone down on the bed and reaches for my hand again. "Officers found him in his room when they searched the inn looking for him. It appears someone shot him in the back."

"Who? Do they have any suspects? Did Mr. Gillman see anything?"

Travis shrugs like it's not a big deal. "The guys are at the inn now questioning everyone. We'll know more once they're done."

I throw the covers off me and attempt to get out of bed.

"Do you need to use the bathroom? I can get the nurse."

I scowl at him and try to remove the needle from my hand, but I'm having trouble getting the tape off. "No, I don't have to use the bathroom. I'm getting dressed. We're going to the inn."

Travis stands quickly and covers my hand with his. "No, Autumn. We're staying right here. The guys will figure this out. You need to rest."

I roll my eyes. "Really, Trav? No offense, but your guys

haven't solved a case in two years, what makes you think they'll solve this one? Even I'm having a hard time figuring out suspects and motives."

Travis frowns and takes my hand in his. "Then let's work it out. Here. Where you can rest."

I open my mouth to protest, but he cuts me off.

"Once we have a list with motives, we'll go from there."

I smile, thinking that I've won.

"That doesn't mean you're leaving this hospital though, Aut." He gives me a knowing look.

I frown and stick out my lower lip.

"Don't even think about giving me that cute pout of yours, it's not going to work," Travis says, turning away from me so he doesn't have to see my puppy dog face.

I smirk because I know it's my secret weapon and the key to getting out of this hospital. Travis has never been able to resist my puppy dog face and I'm hoping that's still the case. I have to get back to the inn and solve this case before the weekend ends and I lose the ability to see things no one else can. I sigh and act resigned. "Fine, you win. Let's make a list." I sit back down on the bed and pull the blankets over my legs.

Travis turns around with a stunned expression on his face. "Really?" Then he narrows his eyes. "You're playing me, aren't you?"

I flutter my eyelashes and hold my hands to my heart. "Why, Captain Mills, I would never."

He rolls his eyes and plops down next to me on the bed. "You're not fooling anyone, Miss Fish-," he pauses then coughs into his hands as his face grows red.

I reach out and pat his arm. "It's fine. I'm probably going to change my name back anyway..." then I remember my tumor or mass or whatever is making a home in my brain and add softly, "if I get the chance to."

Travis whips his head toward me so fast he might have whiplash. "Autumn Marie Fish... Parker, you're going to live. You're going to solve this case. Get through your surgery and go back to running the spa and solving cases the good old-fashioned way. And one day, hopefully in the near future, you'll agree to go out with me and then be my wife. We're going to have those two-beautiful red-headed twins that Lindy wrote about in her journals so don't you dare put out into the universe that anything is going to happen to you. Do you understand me?" His face is beet red and he's huffing and puffing like he can't catch his breath.

I blink back the tears that are threatening to spill from my eyes and take his hand. "Okay."

"Okay?" he asks, then straightens, takes a deep breath and says more matter of fact, "Okay. Yes. You're going to be fine." He kisses my hands then gets up to grab a piece of paper and pen off the cabinet by the window. "Now, let's make a suspect list. I guess we can cross Sloan off."

"Unless he was working with someone and they double crossed him," I suggest.

"Hmm. It's possible, but since Sloan's dead we're also looking for his killer. We'll put him on the suspect list with a line to the side for his killer." Travis jots down his name then asks, "Who else?"

"Mrs. Soggs. Although I'm not sure she would have killed Sloan. She was with us at the café and you said she was at the station as soon as she got into town, right?"

Travis nods. "We'll add her, but I'm not sure she's a good suspect," he says, jotting down her name. "What about Paula?"

"The scorned lover. Yes, definitely." I pause and think

about anyone else who could have had it out for the instructor and/or Sloan. "What about the instructor's fiancée?"

"Ana?"

"Yeah, we need to find more out about her. Maybe she had something to do with these deaths?"

"How? Why? She left the instructor for another guy. She's probably happily married by now."

"Maybe, but I still think we need to locate her. At the very least let her know her ex-fiancée died."

Travis nods. "Alright, I'll have one of the guys look into her once we get a last name from Mrs. Soggs. Anyone else?"

I chew on my lower lip and think about the other people in our group. "What about Olive?"

"She found the body."

"She did, but did she push him before she found him?"

"I don't know, Autumn," Travis says, tapping the pen against his chin.

A gasp comes from the door and we turn to see Olive standing in the doorway.

"How dare you think I would kill the instructor. I would never. I'm a healer, not a killer."

Where have I heard that before? Oh, me. That's what I said when April was murdered. "I'm sorry, Olive. We aren't ruling anyone out. It's nothing personal."

She crosses her arms over her chest. "It most certainly is personal. You're accusing me of murder." She sticks her nose up in the air as if the thought is beneath her.

"Well, did you?"

"Autumn," Travis growls a warning.

"Wow." Olive balls her fists at her sides. "I came to check on you after the instructor's mother said you fainted and this is what I get? You accusing me of murder?"

I bite my lip. "Sorry. No offense. It's just part of our job."

Olive sniffs then wipes her nose. "I understand."

"So, Mrs. Soggs is at the inn?"

"Yes, she showed up right before the police did. I guess she's staying in her son's room. Which is creepy if you ask me. Who does that?"

"Hmm. That is kind of strange. Morbid even, but it is just a room. The last place her son stayed... alive. Maybe it brings her comfort."

Olive shivers. "Or nightmares. I'm so ready to leave that creepy old inn. I can't wait for class to be over tomorrow."

I study her for a moment then ask, "Olive, what were you doing in the kitchen last night?"

She blinks like she isn't sure she heard me correctly then sighs, "I missed dinner because I took a nap after we got back. I was too tired to drive into town so I was looking for a piece of fruit or something to eat. The instructor was doing the same thing before he headed upstairs."

"Did you hear anything after he retreated upstairs? Anyone fighting or some sort of altercation before the instructor fell down the stairs?"

She furrows her brows and doesn't say anything for a moment. "Now, that I think about it there were a couple of raised voices at the top of the stairs. I didn't really pay much attention to it because I was focused on finding food. I was in the pantry when he landed at the bottom of the stairs so the voices were muffled."

"Did it sound like a woman and a man arguing or two males?"

She frowns and closes the door to the room before walking over to the end of the bed to sit down. "I think it was two men. At first I thought it was Sloan and the instructor then I remember seeing Sloan sneaking out the side door when I came into the kitchen."

"Sloan was sneaking out of the inn? Why? He could have just left. No one would have cared."

"I don't think he wanted to be seen. He is… was an odd guy that one. Really sketchy. I looked him up online and found out his license was taken away last year. A woman complained about him and the board investigated it and put him on probation. I don't even know why he was at the class. It's not like these credits will do him any good since he won't get his license back for two years."

"Two years? Really?"

Olive nods. "Yeah, the woman made it sound like he was totally unprofessional. Not draping her properly, making lude comments about her body and even touching her inappropriately."

I gasp. "No."

"Yes. It's her word against his, but the board's taking it very seriously."

"I bet and they should. I wonder why he was here. Who was the woman who made the complaint?"

"They didn't release her name. Obviously for confidentiality reasons."

My gaze flickers to Travis.

Travis meets my eyes, nods and immediately gets up to use his phone. "I'll be right back. Stay with her, okay?"

Olive nods and watches him leave before turning back to me. "He's awfully protective of you. Are you two a thing?"

I quirk an eyebrow. "A thing?"

"You know, an item. A couple. Are you dating?"

"No."

"No? That can't be. He's obviously in love with you."

"We used to date. In high school."

"Ah, high school sweethearts. You never get over that one. They stay with you no matter what or who you date in the future. They always have a piece of your heart." She sighs like she's speaking from experience.

"Well Travis and I are just friends. That's it."

"Ummhmm. I wish I had a friend who looked like him and who cared for me the way he does you. You may be a recent widower, but mark my words, you two will be married and have a baby on the way in the next year."

My heart rate picks up and the monitor beeps beside me.

Olive smirks and pats my leg. "Your secret's safe with me."

I frown at her words.

She smiles at me, but doesn't say anything.

Travis steps back into the room. "Olive, I think it's safer for you to stay at the station."

"The station? Why?"

"You may be in danger at the inn. If the killer thinks you heard or saw them, you could be the next target. I have an officer coming to escort you now."

Olive opens her mouth to protest when an officer pokes his head in the door.

"Ready, Miss?"

Olive glares at Travis before stomping out of the room without even a good-bye.

I can't say I blame her, spending the night at the station isn't ideal, but at least she'll be safe.

Travis sits back down next to me. "It seems we have a connection between Sloan and Tony."

"Really? What?" I sit up straighter in bed and give Travis my full attention.

"They went to the same school together. Their last

known address was even the same. Maybe they were partners."

"Hmm." I tap my chin. "Any luck on finding the woman who made the complaint against Sloan?

He sighs. "Felicia Allen died in a single car crash last week. It seems she was under the influence."

I frown. "That sounds suspicious."

"Or the stress of the case got to her."

"I guess."

"You think Sloan had something to do with it?"

I shrug, not sure what to think.

"Do you think Sloan pushed Tony?" Travis asks, taking a seat at the foot of the bed.

"Olive said Sloan was sneaking out the back door when she came into the kitchen. There's no way he could have pushed the instructor if he was outside."

"Unless he came back in through the front door and snuck up the main staircase. They argue and he pushes the instructor."

I shake my head. "No. Mr. Gillman would have seen him. He was in the den, remember? He was tending to the fire. He said he didn't see Sloan or Olive all night."

"He's old. I'm sure his memory isn't that good anymore. He could have had his back turned when Sloan snuck in."

"There's a bell on the door. He would have heard it." I sigh because I'm starting to get a headache.

Travis frowns. "If Sloan didn't kill the instructor, then who did?"

"I don't know, but I plan to find out."

10

"Wake-up, sleepy head."

I blink then blink again. The sun's streaming in through the hospital window and fills the room with natural light. I glance around and notice a few bouquets of wildflowers sitting on the cabinet by the window. I turn to my right when I feel someone standing next to me. "Josh," I whisper, staring up into his blue eyes.

He smiles and asks, "How are you feeling?"

"I'm fine."

He gives me a look like he knows I'm lying. "You do know I can see and hear everything that's going on, right? I knew about the brain tumor... even before Dr. Gregory did."

I cringe. "Does that mean I'm going to die? Is that why you're here?"

He smiles again. "Autumn, only the big guy upstairs knows the answer to that. I'm here because you need me. You aren't moving on. You're stuck. You still haven't scattered my ashes. Why not?"

I play with the blanket, avoiding his intense stare. "I've been busy."

"Autumn, look at me."

I shake my head because I can already feel the tears bubbling to the surface and I know if I look at him, I'll break. He can't see me break down. He'll never move on if I do. He needs to move on, right?

"Autumn, please look at me," Josh says, softly.

I sigh and shift my eyes to him.

"Why are you not moving on? I know you read my letter. The whole town read my letter. No one's going to judge you if you start dating. All you're doing is working and sleeping. You're surviving, not living. You know I don't want you to live like this."

I open my mouth to protest when he cuts me off.

"If I was alive and you were... not, you'd tell me the same thing."

"But you wouldn't listen," I argue.

He drops his head then shakes it. "True, but you're the love of my life."

I open my mouth again to tell him he's mine when he holds up a hand.

"Don't tell me I'm the love of your life. Yes, I was your best friend. Yes, you loved me, but your heart has always belonged to Travis." He pauses like it pains him to say those words before continuing, "Why are you keeping him at arm's length?"

"I'm not," I object, crossing my arms over my chest in defense.

"Yes, you are. You're scared. I get it, but you shouldn't be. Travis isn't going to hurt you. He loves you. Always has. Not to mention, he's not the same immature kid he was in high school. He will love you. Provide for you. Support you. Love your twins."

I whip my head toward him. "You know?"

He nods. "Of course, I do. I know a lot of things."

"Like who killed Tony Soggs and Sloan Burke?"

He smirks. "Yes."

I sit up in the bed and reach for his hands.

He steps back.

"What's wrong?"

"You can't touch me."

"Why not?"

"I'm a ghost, Autumn."

"Oh, right." I pause. "So, you came here to tell me to move on. Help me with the clue to link Paula and the instructor and now, what? You disappear?"

"Nope."

"Nope? What does that mean?"

"I'm not done here."

I open my mouth to ask what else he needs to do when the door opens and Travis steps inside with a white takeout bag from the café, a smoothie and a white paper coffee cup. My eyes widen because I don't want him to see Josh, but when I look to my right, Josh is gone.

"What's wrong? Are you feeling ok? You're as white as your bed sheets." He rushes to my side, puts down the food and drinks on the table and places a hand to my forehead. "Should I call a nurse?"

I shake my head, brushing off his hand and take a deep breath to calm my racing heart. "No, I'm fine." *Sheesh, I feel like I've been saying that a lot lately.*

"Really? Because you don't look fine. I think I should have Dr. Gregory paged."

I grab his wrist to stop him. "No, please." Then I distract him by asking, "What did you bring me?"

His expression turns from worried to smug. "Ah, so she's hungry."

My stomach growls to second his claim. "Famished."

"You kept telling me last night that you weren't hungry."

"I did?" I frown, trying to remember last night. "The last thing I remember is saying I was going to figure out who killed the instructor."

"So, the sedatives worked?" He says, taking some bagels and containers out of the bag.

I sit up in bed and frown. "Sedatives, what sedatives?"

"I knew you would try to figure out a way to leave the hospital last night so I asked the nurse to put a sedative in your IV."

"When?"

"When you got up to go to the bathroom, right after you told me you were going to find out who killed the instructor."

"You had me drugged?"

He shrugs and hands me a container with some fruit and another one with some oatmeal. "Dr. Gregory thought it was a good idea too."

I snort and cross my arms over my chest.

Travis smirks. "Don't be mad, Aut. I had to go back to the station and we all knew you wouldn't have stayed here. You needed to rest."

I glare at him.

"Eat up." He gestures to the food. "Today's going to be a long day."

"Today? What's happening today?"

"Well for one, your parents will be here later."

"My parents?! You called them. Why? They're just going to worry."

"And they should. You have a tumor in your brain, Autumn. They want to be here for you. Support you. Take care of you."

I groan. "That's not what I want. You know I don't like people fussing over me."

"Well then you're really not going to like that Josh's parents are also coming with them."

I groan again. "No. I can't deal with my parents and his right now. We have a murder to solve."

"And that's another thing you have to do today."

"What?"

"Solve the murder."

"But how am I going to do that if I can't leave the hospital."

Travis takes a bite of his bagel and gestures to my food. "Eat first then we'll talk."

I open my mouth to protest, but he sticks a piece of fruit in it.

"Eat."

I close my mouth and chew. We eat in silence until our plates are clean. I push my container to the side and clasp my hands over my belly. "There, I ate. Now tell me how I'm going to solve this case when I'm stuck here."

He stands and throws away the trash then grabs a duffel bag from the couch. "There's some clothes in here for you to change into."

"Change into?" I narrow my eyes at him. "What's going on, Travis?"

"Dr. Gregory has cleared you to leave."

My eyes light up.

Travis holds up a hand. "Only for today and I have to

have you back in this room by six o'clock tonight so you can get some rest before your surgery." He pauses and studies me. "Do you feel up to this?"

"Of course," I say, reaching for the bag.

He holds it to his chest. "No, not yet."

"What? I thought we were going to solve this case. It's already nine a.m."

"Dr. Gregory said that you are not to use your 'gift' at any point today."

My jaw drops. "What do you mean? I can't solve this case unless I can see who killed the instructor and Sloan."

"You will just have to solve it the old-fashioned way."

"What? Like with clues and stuff?"

He smirks. "Yes, Autumn. Like with clues and stuff."

I roll my eyes and grab the bag from his hand as a brunette nurse in purple scrubs walks in.

"Before you rip that IV out of your hand, let me help you," she says, removing the needle from my hand.

"Thank you," I say, rubbing the bandage and tape she puts over the vein.

She smiles then turns to Travis. "You better take good care of her today. I'm surprised Dr. Gregory is even letting you take her out of here."

I frown and furrow my brow. "Why? I'm fine."

She turns and studies me. "Yes, honey, you'll be fine."

"No really, I'm fine."

She gives me a sympathetic look. "Of course, dear, but please take it easy. Don't push yourself, okay?" Then she turns and leaves.

I turn to Travis. "Am I not okay?"

He shakes his head. "You'll be fine as long as you don't have any visions."

"And if I do? Then what happens?"

Travis looks away from me and runs a hand through his hair.

"Trav, look at me," I demand, balling my fists and feeling tears well up in my eyes, but I blink several times to keep them from falling.

He glances over at me.

"What will happen?" I choke out.

"No one knows. You could pass out. You could have a seizure. You could di…" his voice trails off.

"I could die!" I cry out then burst into tears.

Travis wraps his arms around me and pulls me into him. "Shh. It's okay. You're going to be fine. Just don't touch anyone and stay close to me." He pauses. "You don't have to do this, Aut. We can stay here. You can rest. The guys can solve this case… eventually."

I snort and laugh. "Yeah right." Breathing in his woodsy scent, I focus on trying to slow my breathing. I sniffle and step back from Travis. The thought of having a seizure is scary enough, but dying is a whole different story. I take in Travis's face. The scar on his eyebrow from when he had a bike accident in kindergarten. The freckles across his nose from the sun. His red hair that's in need of a haircut, but shaggy, just the way I like it. His jaw's clenching back and forth and his body's shaking. He's scared and so am I, but I have to do this. I need to do this.

He reaches up and strokes my cheek, wiping away some of my tears. "You're going to be fine. Nothing's going to happen to you. I won't let it. Okay?"

I nod and swallow the lump in my throat.

His eyes bounce back and forth between mine and my lips. He leans down, but then changes his mind at the last minute and whispers, "Get dressed so we can solve this case."

11

"Why are we going to the inn? Isn't everyone at the spa?" I ask, gazing out the window at the pine trees lining the road.

"No, Regina decided to finish the class at the inn." Travis glances at me before returning his gaze to the road. "It will give us a chance to look around for clues. Maybe chat more with Mrs. Soggs... just don't touch her, okay?"

"I know. I know," I sigh, silently berating the tumor in my head. It gave me the ability to see things no one else could and now, I can't even use it to help me solve this case.

We pull up to the inn and Travis gets out to open my door. I take a deep breath to settle my nerves then step out into the humid morning. Going from the air-conditioned car to the heat causes me to shiver.

Travis studies me for a moment before asking, "You ready for this?"

"As ready as I'll ever be," I say, stepping onto the porch.

"Mrs. Parker," Mr. Gillman says, opening the door for me and gesturing for us to come inside. "How are you today?"

I smile at the old man. "Fine, Mr. Gillman. How are you?"

He coughs and wipes his nose with a handkerchief then tucks it into his blue button-down shirt pocket. "Can't complain. Your group's in the formal dining room if you want to join them."

"Oh, well I think we're going to look around for a little bit, if that's okay?"

"Of course," he says, his gaze shifting to the stairs. "I'm going to go check on Mrs. Soggs. She hasn't come down for breakfast yet." He takes off toward the stairs.

Travis and I move into the den. We scan the room, but I'm not exactly sure what we're looking for. It's not like looking around is going to spark anything for me especially since I can't touch anything.

I gasp when Josh appears behind the couch.

"What? What's wrong? Do you feel ok?" Travis is instantly at my side, his eyes searching mine for any sort of distress.

I shake my head. "I'm fine," I reply, my voice quivering as I peer over his shoulder at Josh.

Josh smiles at me then points after Mr. Gillman and mouths, "Follow him."

"Trav, I think we should follow Mr. Gillman."

"What? Why?"

"Just a hunch."

"Alright, let's go have a chat with Mr. Gillman." Travis says, starting toward the stairs.

I hurry behind him and hold onto the banister because I'm feeling kind of light-headed, but there's no way I'm telling Travis. He'll take me back to the hospital and I'll never get a chance to solve this case. At the top of the stairs, we start checking rooms. Most of them are locked, but one is open and Mr. Gillman is whispering on the other side of the door.

Travis opens the door, takes in the room then asks, "Mr. Gillman, who are you talking to and why are you on the floor?"

I peer over Travis's shoulder and notice the room's empty except for Mr. Gillman and he is indeed on the floor. The bed is pushed against the wall and it looks like he's trying to pry up the floorboards.

Mr. Gillman blinks then looks confused. "Talking? I'm not talking to anyone." He drops his tools, stands quickly and swipes his hands down his pants.

Travis glances at me with uncertainty in his eyes. "What's going on here?" Gesturing to the floorboards.

"Oh, um. There's a loose floor board. Mrs. Soggs mentioned it last night so I thought I'd get a jumpstart on fixing it."

"I thought you came up to check on Mrs. Soggs. Where is she?" I scan the room, but don't see her anywhere. In fact, I don't even see a suitcase or any of her belongings.

"Must have gone into town for breakfast." He glances down at the floor board again. "If you'll excuse me, I'd like to get this fixed before she gets back."

"Need some help getting that board up, Mr. Gillman?" Travis asks, stepping toward him.

"No!" He cries then clears his throat. "I mean, no. I've got it. You two have a case to solve. I don't want to trouble you. I've got it."

"Ookay, well holler if you need any help," Travis says, with uncertainty.

Mr. Gillman shoots him a smile and a thumbs up.

I frown because I've never seen Mr. Gillman give anyone a thumbs up. He's acting really strange.

"Come on, Autumn. Let's go look around." Travis motions for me to head out, closing the door behind him once I go through. "Is it just me or is Mr. Gillman not acting like himself?"

"It's not you. He's definitely not acting like himself. Maybe the stress of the inn's getting to him."

"Speaking of stress, how are you feeling?" Travis reaches out to place a hand to my forehead like he's going to check my temperature.

I open my mouth to tell him there's no need to worry when Josh pops up behind him. He smiles and winks at me before pointing to the staircase then disappears. I blink hoping he'll return, but when he doesn't, I turn toward the staircase. The staircase Tony fell down. We already checked it for clues, but maybe we missed something. I move around Travis and head to the stairs.

"Where are you going?" Travis inquires, following close behind. When I don't respond he asks, "Are you ignoring me?"

I roll my eyes because he's hovering and treating me like a child. I know he's worried about me, but I really wish we could go back to how we were before we found out I have a brain tumor. I want to be 'normal' Autumn. Massage Therapist. Solving cases in her spare time. Not this weak light headed, fainting girl that everyone's treating like she's going to break at any moment. "No, Travis. I'm not ignoring you, I'm looking for clues. Care to join me?" I say with a trace of sarcasm in my voice.

He sighs and takes my hands so I have to face him. "I'm sorry, Autumn. I know I'm being a worry wart. I just don't want to lose you. Not when I have you back in my life. I'll try to not smother you as long as you let me know if you're feeling faint or you get a headache or god forbid a vision." He stifles a shudder.

I chew on my lower lip. Is seeing Josh a vision?

"What? Did you have one talking to Mr. Gillman?"

I shake my head.

"Then what? You only chew on your lip when there's something you don't want to tell me."

I sigh. "I've seen Josh."

Travis lets go of my hands and whips around like he's going to see him then turns back to me. "Is he here now?"

"No, but he was in the living room. He told me to follow Mr. Gillman and just now pointed to the stairs."

"The stairs? We already looked at the stairs. The fabric swatch was the only thing we found and it was Tony's. His scrubs had a hole and matched the swatch."

"Well there must be something we missed. Josh wouldn't point to the stairs if there was nothing to find."

We both begin searching the area around the stairs. Something glistens from underneath the table beside the stairs. I crouch down to get a closer look. An earring. "Travis."

"Did you find something?"

I point to the earring and he extracts a glove from his pocket along with an evidence baggy to secure it. "Do you think this has something to do with the case?"

"It could. Definitely points to a struggle."

"It also points to the killer being a woman."

"Men can wear earrings too."

"True, but I haven't seen any men with earrings here this weekend. Have you?"

Travis shakes his head. "I'll take this to the lab for testing."

"Or we could simply ask around and see if anyone's lost an earring," I suggest.

Travis smirks. "Let's go see if we can find ourselves a diamond owner."

"Or better yet... a killer."

12

———

Everyone's still milling around the breakfast table, sipping coffee and chatting amongst themselves when we enter the dining room. They stop talking when they notice us.

Regina gets up and rushes over. "Good morning you two." She turns to me and gives me a sympathetic smile. "How are you feeling, Autumn?"

"As good as can be expected," I confess with a forced smile.

Her eyes glisten with tears before she yanks me into a hug.

I pat her back and struggle to catch my breath due to her suffocating hold on me.

Travis gives her a few more seconds before rescuing me. "Alright, let Aut breathe. I don't need her passing out when there's a case to solve."

Paula pipes up at those words, "So, you found out who killed Tony?" She swipes a strand of hair behind her ear."

"We have a lead, but before we discuss that, has anyone

lost an earring? We found it on the floor upstairs." Travis pulls it out and plops it down on the table.

Anita gasps. "Oh, you found it!" she exclaims. "I've been looking everywhere for it." She reaches out to snatch it, but Travis stops her.

"If you don't mind stepping into the den, we would like to have a word with you."

"Me?" Anita looks confused. "Why me?"

"Mrs. Case, the den please."

Her husband, George stands and pulls out her chair. "It's alright darling. We have nothing to hide. They'll just have a little chat with us then we can finish this class and head home." He tucks her arm in his and starts for the den.

"Actually, Mr. Case. We would like to speak with your wife alone," Travis says, sternly

George blinks then narrows his eyes at Travis. "Whatever you need to say to my wife, you can say to me."

Anita pats his hand. "I'll just be a minute, dear. Finish your coffee and I'll be right back."

George huffs out a frustrated breath, but sits back down mumbling to himself.

Travis raises an eyebrow at me then gestures for Anita to go ahead of him.

She shoots him a tight smile before stomping off to the other room.

I smirk and follow Travis, but as I'm passing the main staircase something catches my eye. A light's shining underneath a small door next to the stairs. I quickly grab Travis by the arm.

"What's wrong? Do you feel ok?" Concern's etched all over his face.

"I'm fine, but look." I point to the light under the door. "What's down there?"

Travis frowns. His gaze bouncing back and forth between the door and the other room. He seems torn about whether or not to check out what's behind the door or to question Anita.

"I'll stay with Anita while you check it out."

"Are you sure?"

I nod. "Go, but be careful."

"Always." His eyes lock with mine for a moment before he rubs the back of his neck and mutters, "You too. I'll be right back."

I nod again as he takes off down the stairs.

"Um, hello? Where did the detective go? I don't have all day," Anita calls from the other room. She's leaning against the door frame with her arms crossed over her black scrubs. Her blond hair is pulled back in a high ponytail and her blue eyes flash with annoyance.

"He's checking something out. He'll be right back. Why don't you get comfortable?"

"Can I have my earring back now?"

I ignore her question and inquire, "Did George give them to you?"

Anita looks away and fiddles with the edge of her scrub top. "No."

"Were they a family heirloom?"

She shakes her head.

I narrow my eyes and study her. "Someone special then?"

"You could say that."

I sigh knowing this interview isn't going anywhere with her lack of answers and decide to change directions. "You went to school with Tony, didn't you?"

Anita's head jerks up and she glares at me. "So?"

"So, were you two close?"

She shrugs.

"Did you know an Ana?"

She stiffens and turns to look out the window.

"It sounds like she and Tony had a great love affair. She broke his heart when she called off their engagement." I pause and study her. She blinks back what I think are tears, but can't tell as she turns away from me. "According to Mrs. Soggs, Ana broke up with him because she fell in love with someone else."

Anita doesn't respond just continues to look out the window.

I continue, "I wonder how someone could accept a ring from one man, but then fall in love with another."

Anita whips her head around. "Relationships are hard, complicated and there are other extenuating circumstances..." her voices trails off as she turns back to the window.

"It sounds like you're speaking from experience."

She doesn't respond.

I open my mouth to ask another question when commotion in the other room draws my attention.

"Let me go."

"Mrs. Soggs, what were you really doing in the basement?"

"I told you I was looking for clues."

"Rita?" Mr. Gillman moves slowly down the stairs. "Where have you been?"

"I was just telling the captain here that I was trying to find clues on who killed my Tony," Mrs. Soggs says, glaring at Travis.

Travis narrows his eyes. "In the basement?"

"It was the only place I hadn't searched yet." Mrs. Soggs

catches sight of Anita. "You! You broke my Tony's heart, probably killed him too." She starts toward her.

Anita gasps and her cheeks flush. "I would never."

"Mrs. Soggs, I have some questions about your son's death," Travis says, stepping in front of her to block her path.

"Not here. Not with her," she sneers. "I'll wait in my room." With that she turns on her heels and storms up the stairs with Mr. Gillman on her heels.

Travis groans and shakes his head before joining me in the den. "Mrs. Case, care to enlighten us on why Mrs. Soggs says you broke her son's heart and why she's accusing you of murder?"

Wringing her hands, Anita turns back to the window, but doesn't say anything.

Travis shoots me a sideways glance then clears his throat and takes a seat on the sofa. "Mrs. Case, where were you around the time Tony Soggs was pushed down the stairs?"

Anita blinks like she can't believe Travis just asked her this. "I-I already gave my statement to an officer the other night."

"I know, but I would like to hear it from you."

Anita crosses her arms over her chest as her eyes dart around the room.

I study her wondering why she's nervous when a vision hits me. I gasp and my legs give out, causing me to drop down on the sofa. I can't control my mind. The vision just comes to me.

Anita and Tony are holding hands. There's a diamond ring on her finger. They're looking at wedding cakes. Anita's phone rings and she steps outside to take it. She says George's name and giggles then looks over her shoulder at Tony through the glass. She hangs up then goes back to looking at cakes with Tony.

I gasp again as the vision dissipates.

"Autumn! Autumn!" Travis is crouching down in front of me with worry etched all over his face. "What happened? Was it a vision?"

Pain shoots through my head and I try to catch my breath. I reach up to rub my temples. The tumor must be growing or putting pressure on my brain because I usually have to touch something to get a vision. This one just came to me out of nowhere. I blink and take another deep breath. "Water," I choke out, thinking that may alleviate the throbbing in my head.

"Don't move. I'll be right back," Travis says, before he races off to the kitchen.

"What's wrong with you?" Anita asks, staring at me like I'm an alien.

"Migraine," I lie although I'm not sure it's a lie because it feels like someone's putting an axe through my skull.

Travis rushes back in with a bottle water and shoves it into my hands. "Here. Drink. Breathe. You're really pale. Maybe you should lie down. I'll call Dr. Gregory. Maybe I should call an ambulance," he rambles, raking a hand through his red hair.

I place a hand on his. "Trav. I'm fine. It's just a little pain. I'm probably dehydrated."

He frowns and studies me before saying, "I still think you should lie down."

I take another swig of water before setting the bottle on the table next to me. "Actually, I would like to speak with Ana."

Anita scoffs. "No one calls me Ana."

"Tony did."

Travis blinks then raises an eyebrow at me before mouthing, 'vision'?

I nod.

His frown deepens, but he turns to Anita. "So, you were Tony's fiancée?"

She shrugs. "It was a mistake."

"A mistake? How so? Because you were also engaged to George? How is being engaged to two men a mistake?"

Anita is in my face within seconds. "Lower your voice," she snaps.

"Oh, George doesn't know?"

Anita sits down next to me and keeps her voice low, "No." She looks down at her wedding ring, which is different than the one I saw in my vision. "George was busy getting our spa up and running. I needed some continuing education credits, so I went to a Craniosacral class in Vegas. Tony was teaching it. As you know, we went to massage school together so we decided to catch up at dinner. Dinner led to drinks. Drinks led to a night cap and well it just kind of happened." She shrugs. "It was a silly fling."

I raise an eyebrow even though it feels like it weighs a hundred pounds. "A fling that turned into an engagement?"

"Tony was persistent." She sighs then continues, "He kept calling and texting. George was preoccupied with the spa and I was feeling lonely and vulnerable. I didn't mean to fall for Tony, it just happened. I was going to call off the wedding with George."

"So, why didn't you?"

"George could tell I wasn't happy so he surprised me with a weekend getaway. I figured I owed it to him to hear him out before breaking up with him."

"But it didn't happen that way?"

Anita shakes her head and smiles. "No. We reconnected and I knew he was the man I was supposed to marry. I mean we were opening a business together. He was trying to make everything perfect and he did."

"What about Tony?"

A tear falls from Anita's eye and she swipes it away. "I broke up with him. He didn't take it well."

I chew on my lip, mulling over everything Anita's told me. "So why sign up for this class? You knew it would upset Tony, right?"

Anita looks down at her wedding ring again. "I didn't, George did. He needed some more continuing education credits for his license and thought it would be a nice getaway for us."

"Did Tony approach you?"

"He tried, but George was always with me. Tony asked me to meet him the night he died, but George would barely leave my side so I never got to meet up with him."

"How did your earring end up at the top of the stairs?"

Anita fiddles with her earlobe. "The back is always coming out. I lost it the first day we were here. Before Tony... well before he fell. I've been looking for it all weekend. I thought it was lost forever. It's the only thing I have left of Tony." She sighs. "It would probably be better if it stayed lost. I'm married, I need to move on. I love my husband. Really, I do," she says it like she's trying to convince herself more than us.

Travis types something into his phone then asks, "So, George was with you all night?"

"Um, no. He went to get me some water. I thought I could slip out to meet Tony, but my mom called. We talked for about ten minutes or so before I heard Olive scream." Anita's eyes fill with tears.

"Are you sure George didn't know about you and Tony?" I inquire, rubbing my temples.

Anita shakes her head. "Yes. Absolutely. There's no way. I never told him. George is extremely possessive and jealous. He would murd..." her voice trails off and her eyes grow wide.

"Murder?" Travis asks, his eyes darting to the dining room. "Do you think George would murder Tony if he found out about the affair?"

"I-I" before she can finish her statement there's a commotion in the dining room and someone screams.

13

———

"**S**tay here," Travis orders before he takes off toward the dining room.

"What's going on?" Anita inquires, scooting closer to me.

"I'm not sure." I move to get up, but she latches onto my arm.

"Wait! Where are you going? He told us to stay put."

"It'll be fine. You stay. I'll go." I pat her hand and pry her fingers off my arm before dashing toward the dining room. Before I can open the door, Regina comes rushing out. I grab her arm and pull her over to the wall. "What's happening in there?"

"She's gone mad!" She exclaims.

"Who?"

Regina's face is red and her eyes are wide like she's in shock. "That quiet girl."

"Olive?"

"Yes, Her. She's swinging a knife around and spouting things about how everyone's against her."

"What? Why? What started all of that?"

"That Paula girl was making comments about everyone's business. I guess Olive's is struggling and Paula provoked her. She grabbed a knife and lunged at Paula. She started screaming about how hard it is to break into the market and get clients. She's really off her rocker."

I frown, trying to think back to my discussions with Olive. She never mentioned that she was struggling. I mean it's just her in her practice, but that doesn't mean she can't have a successful business. "What else did she say?"

"Huh?" Regina blinks like she's still in shock.

I shake her slightly to jar her out of it. "Regina, focus. What else did she say?"

"Oh, um not much."

"Nothing else?"

"Oh, well she did say that the instructor guy believed in her. He was going to make sure her business took off, but now that he's dead there would be no way for her to succeed."

"What? How was Tony going to get her business to take off? He didn't even live in the same town."

Regina shrugs. "Beats me. The girl's loony. I think all the stress of running a business then the stress of finding a dead body and staying all night at the police station caused her to snap."

Before I can say anything else, the door to the dining room opens and Travis is escorting Olive toward the door. "Wait!" I call out to him and take a step toward them when another vision fills my head.

Olive and Tony are sitting at the kitchen table at the inn, talking about going into business together. He's tucking a strand of hair behind her ear and she's blushing. George comes down the stairs and nods to them before heading to the fridge and grabbing a bottle of water. As he's getting ready to leave, Paula walks in and starts yelling at Tony about cheating on her with Ana and now, he's moving on with Olive. George stiffens and glares at Tony when he hears Ana's name. Tony smirks at him. George balls his fists then stomps back up the stairs. Paula slaps Tony then leaves the room. Olive runs to grab Tony an ice pack, but Tony excuses himself and heads up the stairs.

"Autumn!"

I blink and then blink again. Travis is in my face and for some reason I'm on my knees in the middle of the floor.

"Was it a vision? Is it your head? What's wrong?" Travis is gripping my hands and his face is laced with concern.

"Yes," I squeak.

"Here." Regina squats down and hands me a bottle of water.

I take it and chug it all down before handing it back to her. "Thank you," I choke out.

"Autumn, I'm taking you back to the hospital. That's two visions in less than ten minutes. Something's wrong. You haven't even touched anything."

My eyes fill with tears because I know something's wrong, but we're so close to solving this case. I can't leave now. What if the killer gets away because we can't figure out who killed Tony and Sloan? I would never forgive myself. I know after Dr. Gregory removes this tumor, I'll no longer have visions and I don't know what that means for my sleuthing career. I feel like I have the upper hand with these visions. Without them, I'm not sure.

"Don't cry, Autumn. It's going to be ok." Travis swipes at the tears falling from my eyes.

I blink them back and take in everyone standing around me. "Olive, were you dating the instructor?"

Her face turns bright red as both Anita and Paula glare at her. "Um, no. We were just discussing going into business together. He was rather charming though. Maybe it would have turned into something more." She looks down at her hands and her eyes fill with tears.

"Paula, you thought Tony was dating Olive, didn't you?"

Paula looks everywhere, but at me.

"That made you angry since he'd already cheated on you with another woman, right?"

She doesn't respond so I move onto the next suspect.

"George, you knew about the affair, didn't you?"

His face turns red and he balls his fist much like he did in my vision.

Anita gasps. "You knew?"

He glares at her. "Of course, I knew. You were distant and always taking off to do something while I was busy trying to get our spa up and running. I followed you. I can't believe you agreed to marry that slime ball," he sneers.

"Hey," Paula objects. "He was not a slime ball."

George sneers at her. "Yes, he was. He cheated thousands of dollars out of people. Anita or should I call you Ana, a name you always told me you hated, but I guess it was ok for him to call you that."

Anita looks down at the floor, but doesn't say anything.

George continues, "The only reason Tony latched onto you was because you're rich."

Anita's head snaps up and she glares at George. "He didn't know about my money."

"Oh yes, he did. I didn't just follow you. I followed him."

Anita frowns. "Followed him where?"

"To his place of business." George eyes Travis and mutters, "I kind of broke in. He had a file on you, Anita. He had files on all of us. Our businesses. Bank information. Everything. He knew about each and every one of us and there were also plans on what he planned to do with our businesses."

"What do you mean?" I inquire, stepping closer to George to see if I can get a read on what he's talking about.

"Autumn, he planned to buy your spa. He wanted to franchise all of our businesses. Offer us basically pennies for our businesses then turn them into these elaborate spas."

I frown. "But I would never sell."

George studies me for a moment then continues, "There was a plan for that too."

"What do you mean?" Travis demands, stepping closer to me as if he's concerned about whatever George might say.

George's eyes move to Travis. "He had a partner. First, they were going to destroy the businesses reputation. Make the owner out to be crazy, scare customers away and if that didn't work..." George runs a finger across the front of his throat.

Anita gasps then narrows her eyes at George. "Tony would never do that."

"I have all the proof on my phone." George whips out his phone from his pocket and taps a few things before handing it to Travis. "I think his partner was Sloan."

Travis takes it and scrolls while I try to read over his shoulder. "Why didn't you take this to the police?"

"I wanted to see what he did this weekend. Collect more evidence. Make sure he would be put away for a long time."

Travis punches a few more things on the phone. "I emailed these to myself." He hands the phone back to George. "Did you confront him about any of this?"

He sighs. "No."

"Really? A witness saw you arguing with Tony at the top of the stairs shortly before he took a nose dive down them."

Travis says, crossing his fingers behind his back. He's baiting George to see what he confesses.

George sighs and swipes a hand through his hair. "Tony confronted me. I was headed back to our room and he began to taunt me about his affair with Anita. We argued, I accused him of using her. I didn't tell him that I knew about his plan, though. Then we went our separate ways."

"You didn't take a swing at him? Didn't push him?"

George shook his head. "It wasn't worth it. That guy would have sued in an instant or pressed charges. I've worked too hard to throw everything away for a cheap punch."

Travis nods.

"Why do you think Sloan was his partner?" I inquire, stepping closer to George to see if a vision hits me. I'm surprised nothing comes to me with all this information he's sharing. I take a deep breath and try to focus. It's probably not the smartest thing, but I feel like we need a break in this case.

"I saw the two of them meeting up at his office one day. They were arguing then Sloan shows up here. It seems suspicious."

Travis glances around the room before his eyes fall back on me as if to ask if I'm getting anything.

I shake my head slightly, he seems relieved. Probably because my visions still scare him. "So, you think Sloan killed Tony?"

George shrugs. "Maybe."

"If that's the case then who killed Sloan?"

"Beats me. Sloan was different. Always kept to himself and he was always getting into trouble. He really didn't have the massage therapist vibe if you ask me. The guy was anything but a healer. He was slimy just like Tony."

Anita bursts into tears then rushes up the stairs.

George shakes his head and sighs. "Are we done here? I should go check on her."

Travis nods and motions for him to go.

An officer comes in and takes Olive outside.

"I'm going to go question Mrs. Soggs," Travis says with a sigh. "Why don't you sit down and rest for a minute."

I force a smile. "Mkay."

He studies me for a moment before squeezing my shoulder and jogging up the stairs.

I blink to find just Regina left in the room. "Where did Paula go?"

Regina looks around. "I-I don't know. She was here just a minute ago."

"We need to find her," I say, as a gunshot rings out through the house.

14

Regina grips my arm. "Was that a…"

"It came from upstairs." My eyes widen. "Travis." I start for the steps when Josh appears and shakes his head. "Why?" I mouth to him.

"Just stay, Autumn," he whispers back to me.

A chill runs down my spine and I shiver.

"Are you cold, dear?" Regina asks, wrapping an arm around me and rubbing her hand up and down my arm as if she can keep me warm. "I'm sure Travis is fine. Maybe it was just a sonic boom or something."

I give her a doubtful look, but keep my mouth shut.

"Are you sure you're feeling okay?" She reaches up and checks my forehead as if she thinks I'm running a fever. "Oh, Autumn, you feel kind of warm. I think we should take you back to the hospital."

I wave her off and step to the side. "I'm fine. Really. We have to figure out who the killer is before…"

Travis comes down the stairs with Mr. Gillman in handcuffs.

"What's going on?"

"Mr. Gillman shot Paula."

"What? Why?"

"Because she killed Tony and Sloan. She admitted to it," Mr. Gillman yells through his tears. "And she was trying to kill Anita."

Regina gasps.

"What happened?" I ask, completely confused because even though Paula was high on my suspect list, I didn't actually get the feeling she killed Tony... maybe Sloan, but definitely not Tony.

"She came upstairs spouting off about all the ways Tony wronged her and even Sloan. I guess those two have history. Then she started yelling at Anita about how it was all her fault Tony broke up with her. Paula lunged at her and tried to choke her. I grabbed my rifle to try and scare her, but it just went off. I didn't mean to..." Mr. Gillman breaks down as Travis hands him off to another officer.

"So Paula's... dead?"

Travis nods. "It's not a pretty sight."

"Where's Anita? Mrs. Soggs? George?"

"Upstairs with Officer Kline. They're giving their statements."

I chew on my lip for a moment before asking, "I get why Paula killed Tony, but why Sloan?"

Travis shrugs. "I guess we'll never know."

"But this can't be it. We have to keep investigating."

"Aut, Mr. Gillman said Paula admitted to the killings. Sometimes people do things that don't make sense. Pushing Tony down the stairs was impulsive. She wasn't thinking. Maybe Sloan was going to turn her in so she killed him."

I furrow my brow and glance at the stairs. "Can I go up there?"

"I don't think that's a good idea. It's a bloody mess. I think we should get you back to the hospital. You're looking kind of pale."

"Yes, I agree with Travis." Regina says, patting my arm. "She was shivering a moment ago and feels kind of warm."

Travis frowns and reaches out to check my forehead. "You're burning up. Let's go."

"But..." I protest, still looking at the stairs. Something doesn't feel right. This whole case has been a disaster. I know that if I can just touch Paula, I'll know whether or not she killed Tony and/or Sloan.

"No but's Aut. Your parents should be here soon and tomorrow's going to be a long day for you. You need your rest."

Josh appears behind Travis and nods too.

"Fine," I mutter, knowing Travis isn't going to let me investigate anymore when he thinks the case is closed. Maybe Josh knows something I don't. Maybe Paula was the killer. How did I miss it? I should have gotten a read on that a lot sooner.

Tony's mother comes sniffling down the stairs. Blood's covering the front of her shirt. "He was only trying to protect us. Who knows what she would have done to us. That awful woman killed my son. You can't put him in jail because he did your job," she yells.

"What's going on? Why are you arresting him?" George growls, coming down the stairs with Anita close behind him.

"It's just protocol. Once we have all the evidence, we'll release him," Travis assures them.

George let's out an exasperated sigh then asks, "Are we free to leave now?"

Travis nods. "Yes. We'll contact you if we have any follow

up questions," he says before escorting Mr. Gillman from the room.

Mrs. Soggs rolls her eyes and stomps back up the stairs, muttering under her breath.

Anita turns to me and says, "Well, it was a pleasure meeting you, Autumn. I wish it were under more pleasant circumstances."

I shoot her a smile.

George turns to Regina. "You can just email us our certificates of completion." He hands Regina a card.

She takes it with a nod. "Of course, I'll send them out tomorrow."

George smiles at me then gestures for his wife to head back upstairs.

"Well that was an eventful weekend," Regina exclaims, clasping her hands together. "Let's get you back to the hospital, shall we? I know Travis probably wants to drive you, but I'm sure he won't mind if I do. He probably needs to wrap up a few more things around here before he can leave."

I frown and glance around the room. I'm not quite ready to leave yet. I'm missing something. Something important. I don't believe Paula killed Tony or Sloan. Yes, she was upset with Tony, but she loved him and where does Sloan fall into all of this? Why kill him? My head starts to pound again and bile rises up in my throat. I rush to the waste basket and throw up.

"Autumn, oh my." Regina holds my hair back while shouting for Travis.

"What? What's wrong?" Travis demands, rushing into the room. "Autumn, I'm calling an ambulance. Hang in there."

By the tone of his voice, I know this is serious. I

shouldn't be throwing up like this. Is that blood? I gag again. My head feels like it could explode any minute. Then I feel light-headed and everything goes black.

15

Am I dead?

I watch as Dr. Gregory operates on me. His face is etched with concern. I can only see my face as they work on my brain behind a curtain. Personally, I'm not interested in seeing what the tumor looks like. Then suddenly, I'm floating. Out of the operating room and down the hallway.

When I reach the waiting room, I see my parents, Josh's parents, Travis, Regina, Cat and some of the Crafty Crew ladies. My mom's sitting in a chair dabbing her eyes while Josh's mom tries to console her. My dad's pacing the room, but stops when Travis and Mr. Parker approach him. Travis runs a hand through his hair and mumbles something to my dad. Regina and Cat are huddled together. Cat's crying and Regina's trying to reassure her that I'll be okay. The Crafty Crew ladies look like they're knitting a blanket. They all have a section of fabric and are stitching it together.

Then I'm moving again. Down the hall until I reach the morgue. That's when I see him. "Josh!" I exclaim and move toward him.

He grins. "I've missed you, Autumn."

"I miss you too," I cry.

"Come on, we don't have much time, we have to solve this case."

"What? What do you mean? Paula confessed."

Josh scowls. "Paula didn't confess to anything."

"But Mr. Gillman said she…"

Josh holds up a hand to silence me. "Mr. Gillman lied, Autumn and so did Mrs. Soggs, George and Anita."

"What? Why?"

"Let's go." Josh disappears through the door to the morgue.

I follow him, feeling strange as I pass through the metal door. "What are we doing?" I whisper yell even though I have no clue why. No one can hear me.

Josh smiles and motions to Paula. Her body's lying on the table while her spirit stares down at it.

"Paula," I whisper.

She turns and stares at us. "I didn't kill them."

"Then who did?"

"I heard them."

"Who?"

"Tony's mom and Mr. Gillman."

"What did they say?"

"They were talking about money."

"Money? What money?"

"Money, they stole."

"Stole?" I look to Josh for confirmation.

He nods.

"Mr. Gillman's a thief?"

"Mr. Gillman's dead," Josh whispers.

I gasp. "What?"

Suddenly, we're all three at the inn. Mr. Gillman's spirit is sitting on the sofa staring at the clock.

"Mr. Gillman?"

He turns and nods. "Hi, Autumn. Are you dead too?"

I look at Josh.

He shakes his head. "You're in limbo, if you will."

"But I could die?"

His gaze doesn't meet my eyes so I know there's a chance. I decide to not think about it because we're on a time crunch and I need to solve this case before... well I just need to solve it. Even if I die. I have to know. "Mr. Gillman, what happened? I literally just saw you be taken away in handcuffs."

"That wasn't me. I've been dead for about a week now."

"A week?! Then who is the guy that looks just like you running the inn?"

"Mr. Soggs."

"He's alive?"

Mr. Gillman nods. "Alive and sitting in jail at the moment, but the judge is already signing off to get me... or him out."

"How did they... why did they..."

"Kill me?"

"Um, yes," I say, trying not to sound insensitive.

"Because I found their money. I saw Mr. Soggs... Anthony hiding it one day when I came in their room to change out the linens. I pretended like I didn't see it, but he knew I did. He shot me in my sleep then threw my body in the lake."

I gasp. "Y-You're in the lake... behind your house?"

Mr. Gillman sighs. "Unfortunately, yes and I'm stuck here until someone finds my body and my killer. I guess that's just how it works. Unfinished business and all that stuff."

"I'm so sorry."

"Me too, dear, but it's for the best. The inn was going to be the death of me anyway. I'm just ready to move on." He glances around. "Wherever that may be."

"I'll make sure we retrieve your body and bring your killer to justice as soon as I'm back in my body."

"Autumn, I don't mean to interrupt, but we don't have much time," Josh says, gesturing to the stairs.

"What do you mean? Didn't we solve the case? Mr. and Mrs. Soggs killed Mr. Gillman, I'm guessing their son too although that seems pretty monstrous of them, then Sloan found out so they killed him too. Paula must have just been their scape goat." I turn to Paula. "Right?"

She shakes her head. "No, I overheard them talking about Mr. Gillman. Mrs. Soggs was worried his body was going to resurface and they would get caught. They were devising their next plan. Selling the inn and skipping town."

I frown. "Did they say anything about Tony's murder or Sloan's?"

"No. Mrs. Soggs seemed genuinely upset by his death and even Sloan's. She was crying last night in her room. I heard her through the wall."

"Hmm. Well maybe she didn't kill him, but Mr. Soggs did?"

"Remember Mr. Gillman..." Josh pauses and shoots the real Mr. Gillman a sympathetic look before continuing, "Mr. Soggs said he was in the living room at the time of Tony's murder. The Cases saw him when they retreated up the stairs."

"Yes, but then George went downstairs to get Anita some water and Tony followed him back up the stairs. It would have given Mr. Soggs plenty of time to leave the living room and head upstairs."

"But why push his son down the stairs? It doesn't make any sense," Paula says, glancing around the room. "Where's Tony? Or Sloan? Surely, they haven't crossed over yet."

"Maybe he's upstairs," I suggest, hurrying up the stairs with Josh, Paula and Mr. Gillman on my heels. We stop in front of the room Tony was staying in for the weekend.

"This is the room where Mr. and Mrs. Soggs stayed for their anniversary weekends. Or I guess it wasn't really their anniversary, just a great place to hide all the money they stole from people."

I turn to him. "They hid it in the floorboards underneath the bed, didn't they?"

"Ah, I knew you'd figure it out," Mr. Gillman says with a grin.

"Yeah, he was acting strange and you've never given anyone a thumbs up in your life."

He chuckles. "I'm not a thumbs up kind of guy."

I smile at him then ask, "How did they con people?"

Josh smirks. "Pretending to be ghosts."

"What do you mean?"

"Well you can see how good Mrs. Soggs is at costume make-up. She pretends she's a medium and speaks to the dead. It's usually females who want to talk to their deceased husbands, but sometimes she'll even play the ghost role of a dead wife. She finds a picture of their loved one who's passed and works her magic."

I gasp. "That's awful."

"Yep. They've made a fortune preying on people's grief. They're wanted in about fifteen different states."

I chew on my lip for a moment. "Did Tony know about their scams?"

Josh nods. "He did, but they never included him in their schemes. So, he decided to branch out. Everything George said was true. Tony was going to destroy your business. Make you look like you were a crazy person."

I scoff. "How was he going to do that?"

"By telling everyone you talk to dead people," Tony says, slipping through the closed door.

I laugh. "Everyone in town already knows about my visions. I wasn't the only one in town who had them either. You grossly underestimate this town. Everyone looks out for each other and supports each other, no matter how odd they may be."

Tony huffs. "I figured that out pretty quickly so I moved on to my next target."

"Who? Olive?"

"Olive was like putty in my hand. She couldn't wait to turn her business over to me, but she wasn't going to make me any money. If anything, she was going to be a pawn in my plan."

"And what was I?" Paula demands, crossing her arms over her chest.

"You were supposed to be my wife."

Paula frowns. "Your wife? But you broke up with me... for Ana... Anita."

"Anita was the target. She's loaded. I was planning to marry her, take her for everything she was worth then find you and we would head to Mexico. She had enough money for us to live on for the rest of our lives. Then she broke up with me for that geek George."

Paula swoons. "You were going to come back for me? Marry me?"

"Of course, babe. You're it for me... or were until well..."

"So how was Olive going to be a pawn in your plan?"

"She was going to set up George so Anita would think he was cheating on her."

I roll my eyes. "Olive never would never do anything like that."

"You'd be surprised what people will do when they're desperate. Olive was on the verge of losing everything."

"So, what happened up here?" I gesture to the stairs. "How did you end up..."

"Dead?"

"Well yes."

Tony scratches his head. "I'm not really sure. I remember coming up the stairs. I was going to confront George about Anita's and my affair. I thought maybe if he knew she cheated, he would leave her and I could move forward with my plan. Pretend I was going to help Anita get her spa up and running then divorce her, take the money and run."

I narrow my eyes at him. "What is wrong with you?"

Tony shrugs. "It's how I was raised. Look at my parents. It's just what we do."

"You could be better. Do better."

"It's not in my blood, sweetheart. Paula understands me, don't you babe?"

Paula blushes and giggles then heads over to stand by Tony. "I'd go anywhere with you."

I roll my eyes. "Alright love birds. Let's get back on track. Did you talk to George?"

"I did. The conversation got heated, but I wasn't telling him anything he didn't already know. He was angry, but didn't push me and I saw Ana in the room. She was sitting on the bed talking on the phone when he slammed the door in my face."

"Then what happened?"

"I was going to head back downstairs and talk to Olive. I

heard the floorboards creak, then someone pushed me from behind. That's all I remember."

"So you never saw their face?"

Tony shakes his head. "Nope."

"What about after you died? Did you see anything?"

"There was no one in the hallway when I left my body."

I bite my lip and contemplate the suspects. "Paula, you said you didn't push Tony, right?"

Paula gasps. "I would never. I love him," she gushes, fluttering her eyelashes at him.

Tony grins at her. "I know you wouldn't, babe."

"Paula, George, Anita, Olive and Mrs. Soggs are all out. So that leaves Mr. Soggs..."

"My father wouldn't kill me. He needed me."

"For what?"

"Another scheme he was planning. I was a crucial part of it."

"Maybe the plans changed."

Tony frowns. "H-He's my father. There's no way he would kill me."

"Well then that leaves..."

"Me."

16

We all turn to find Sloan's ghost hovering next to the window.

"You killed Tony?"

Sloan nods.

Tony starts toward him. "How could you? We're brothers."

I gasp. "You're related?"

Tony tries to take a swing at Sloan, but it goes right through him.

"Half-brothers," Sloan says, smirking at Tony's attempts to pummel him. "Dude, you do realize I can't feel a thing, right?"

Tony stops, huffs and crosses his arms. "You're a punk. Why did you kill me?"

"Because you're an idiot." Sloan yawns like he's bored of this conversation.

"I'm an idiot? You're the idiot. Always getting in trouble with the law. Groping that client. What were you thinking? Then you drugged her and put her in a car so it looked like she was driving under the influence. You're a disaster."

Sloan balls his fists and puffs out his chest. "I take risks. It's more than I can say for you. Mom was always raving about you and your petty crimes. I mean marrying a rich girl? Really? How lazy can you be?"

"It was going to be a huge payout. Set me up for life."

"Yeah and leave all of us high and dry. Your dad didn't know you were going to back stab them and run off with your little side piece over here, did he?" he asks, gesturing to Paula.

"Hey, don't talk about her like that," Tony snaps.

Paula smiles at Tony then glares at Sloan. "You're a jerk."

Sloan shrugs. "At least I wasn't planning to sell our family out to save my own skin. You were going to tell the police about what your dad did. Our parents would have gone to jail for killing him." Sloan gestures to Mr. Gillman. "Then what would happen? You would be living the life in Mexico and I would be here doing what? I couldn't let you break up our family. We're in this together."

Tony's face turns red and he looks like he wants to say something, but spins around and storms into his room. Paula follows him.

"Wow, killing your brother." I shake my head and glance at Josh.

He shrugs then looks behind me. "Autumn, you need to hurry up."

"What? Why?" I spin around, but don't see anything.

"Dr. Gregory's finishing up. You don't have long."

I want to ask more questions, but decide I have to find out who killed Sloan. "Do you know who killed you?"

Sloan shakes his head. "I was packing my bag to leave. Mom figured out I killed Tony and told me to leave before my step dad figured it out. He would kill me. We never really got along. Tony was always his favorite."

"Do you think he figured it out?"

"Nah, when I left my body, he was at the lake ensuring this guy wasn't floating to the surface." He gestures to Mr. Gillman again.

Mr. Gillman huffs and disappears.

"What's his problem?" Sloan inquires.

"He's having a hard time with being stuck here. He's ready to move on, but since no one's found his body or his murderer, he can't," Josh tells him. "I'll go check on him. Hurry, Autumn."

"Is there anyone else who would want you dead? Paula said she didn't kill you. It wasn't your mom or your step dad. That leaves Olive, George and Anita."

"It could have been any of them. They were all in their rooms, but I didn't see anyone stashing a murder weapon."

"Hmm...." Before I can say anything else, Josh reappears.

"Autumn, it's time."

"Time? Time for what?"

"Dr. Gregory's finished." Then Josh frowns.

"What? What's wrong?" My body tingles and I feel like I'm fading away. "Josh, what's happening?"

"You're crashing."

"Crashing? Like dying?"

"Fight Autumn. It's not your time."

"But I could stay with you."

He shakes his head. "No, you have to go back. You have to live. For Travis. For Cat. For your parents. For mine. For those future twins. Live Autumn. Live."

Josh gets further away and I struggle to get back to him. "Josh! Don't leave me!"

"Autumn, go back. I'll always be with you. I love you." Josh blows me a kiss then disappears.

Everything goes dark then I hear a voice.

"Autumn? Can you hear me?"

I blink and try to focus. A bright light's shining in front of me.

Am I dead?

Is this heaven?

I blink again and Dr. Gregory's face comes into view.

His face relaxes and he smiles. "You gave us quite a scare. How are you feeling?"

I try to sit up, but a nurse holds me down.

"Relax, Autumn. Just breathe." He pats my hand then checks my bandage. "We were able to remove the entire tumor. I've sent it off to determine if it's cancerous. We should know in a few days." He pulls a light pen from his pocket and shines it in my eyes. "Good. Can you move your fingers? Your toes?"

I wiggle everything and go through a few more tests before Dr. Gregory leaves me to rest. I close my eyes and let the tears fall. I should be grateful that I'm alive, but the tumor's gone, which means I'm never going to see Josh again.

"Aut?"

I open my eyes and see Travis holding a bouquet of sunflowers.

"How are you feeling?"

"Tired."

He smiles and sets the bouquet down on the table by the window before sitting down next to me on the bed. "Your parents are eager to see you, but were kind enough to let me come back first. I think they were afraid I would go bald if I stayed in that waiting room any longer." He gestures to his hair, which looks like he just rolled out of bed.

I laugh, but grab my head when pain shoots through it.

"What? What's wrong? Do I need to call a nurse?"

"No, I'm fine… I think." I take a deep breath and the pain subsides.

"Dr. Gregory said the surgery went well, but he almost lost you." He grabs my hand and holds it to his heart. "I don't know what I would do if I lo-" his voice catches in his throat then he clears it. "If I lost you."

I smile at him. "Trav, I'm okay."

He kisses my palm and mumbles into it, "I was so scared, Aut."

A knock on the door draws our attention.

"Oh, sorry, are we interrupting something?" My mother says, coming into the room with tons of colorful balloons. She sets them down next to the flowers Travis brought and smooths down the front of her floral sundress before coming over to sit next to my bed.

My father dressed in his golfing clothes moves to the other side of the bed and leans down to kiss me on the forehead. "How are you feeling, lady bug?"

"Like someone cut open my head."

My mother cringes, but my dad chuckles. He always appreciates my directness.

"I'll give you two some time with her," Travis says, squeezing my hand then standing up so my mother can sit next to me. "I'm just going to check in with the station. I'll be right outside." He points to the other side of the wall.

"Wait!" I call out to him, causing my mother to jump. "I know who killed Tony."

Travis freezes and turns around slowly. "Y-you do? How? Who?"

I start from the beginning and tell them everything that happened while I was in surgery. When I'm done, all three of them stare at me like I just told them I was moving to France.

"Mr. Gillman's dead?" Travis asks, his brows pinching together.

"Yes, and he's stuck at the inn until his body is found and his killer is brought to justice."

My parents and Travis exchange concerned glances.

"You don't believe me, do you?" I can feel my cheeks growing red and my heart rate increases causing the machine next to me to begin beeping wildly.

A nurse rushes in and shoos everyone out of the room, berating them for upsetting me.

My mother protests.

Travis stutters his way through trying to explain himself.

My father doesn't say a word as he ushers my mother out of the room.

I cross my arms over my chest and refuse to even look at them. Tears drip from my eyes. Where's Josh? Mr. Gillman? I glance around the room and no one shows their face or I guess I can't see them anymore. I close my eyes and try to think about the case.

If Sloan killed his half-brother, Tony, and Mr. Soggs killed Paula then who killed Sloan? And why were George, Mrs. Soggs and Anita backing Mr. Soggs story about Paula confessing to the murders and strangling Anita? Paula didn't even mention attacking Anita. That means they made it up, but why? I think back to what Sloan told me after he died. He said Olive, George and Anita were all in their rooms. Mrs. Soggs was trying to get Sloan to leave before Mr. Soggs found out he killed Tony, but she was also at the café meeting us for dinner and so was Paula. Mr. Soggs was at the lake so if he didn't kill him then who did and why?

Olive didn't really know Sloan. George and Anita went to school with him and Tony, but what motive did they have to kill him? My head starts to hurt so I let myself rest.

When I wake-up, I'm no longer in the hospital.

17

———

I blink and try to figure out where I am. It's dark with only slivers of light coming through the floorboards. It's hot and sticky and I'm still in my hospital gown. My head hurts and I fight the urge to fall back asleep. Maybe I'm dreaming. I close my eyes and take a deep breath, but when I open them again, I'm still in the same place. I hear water lapping against the boards and spot a familiar sign on the wall. I gasp, figuring out where I am. I'm at the inn, in the boat shack, but what am I doing here?

Voices come closer and I strain to hear what they're saying. It's a man and a woman. Is it Mr. and Mrs. Soggs or George and Anita? They're too far away for me to recognize them.

Another wave hits the dock, causing me to jump. The wind rattles the shack and seems like it could crash around me at any moment. A storm must be blowing in. The air's thick and it's hard to breathe. My gown's sticking to my skin and my hair's matted to my forehead. Who took me out of the hospital and how and why?

A car starts up and peels out of the driveway.

I try to sit up and realize my hands are tied together in front of me and so are my ankles. Why would someone kidnap me? It doesn't make any sense. Why wouldn't Mr. and Mrs. Soggs just take the money and run? And whoever killed Sloan could just leave. Paula took the blame for the murders so the police have all but closed the case.

Someone fiddles with the lock outside the door. I hold my breath. The door swings open and a shadow fills the doorway. I squint against the light streaming in behind them. "Wh-who's there?"

The person doesn't say anything and slams the door shut, locking it behind them.

"Wait! Help! Don't leave me here!" I cry out, but it doesn't do any good.

A chainsaw starts up and the shack moves slightly then it's floating or rather sinking.

I gasp. Someone cut the shack off the dock and now I'm going to join Mr. Gillman at the bottom of the lake. Water starts seeping into the cracks. I work at the ropes, but can't get them undone. I begin to panic as water spills in. When the water hits my shoulders, I take a deep breath and try not to think about the fact that it may be my last.

As I go under, I squirm against the ropes, but they don't budge. Drowning is not how I envisioned dying. When I was in high school, I wanted to die in my sleep holding Travis's hand when we're both one hundred and one. Our children would be grown and married with children. We'd have lived a full and happy life together. Now, that's never going to happen. I'm going to be eaten by fish or some other lake creature. I shudder at the thought. I try not to lose hope. I mean Travis is probably out looking for me right now. There's no way I go missing in this town and he not know about it. It's like he has a sixth sense about me. We're connected. Bonded in some way. I close my eyes and focus on Travis. I think about where I am and that I'm in trouble.

My lungs are already screaming and if I don't get air soon this will be it. The shack hits the bottom of the lake and the sides fall apart around me. It's amazing the rotted wood stayed together this long. Once the last of the boards fall, I see Mr. Gillman's lifeless body tied around a bunch of rocks. He's got a gash on his forehead and a bullet wound in his chest. Fish are nibbling on his flesh causing me to gag. My heart aches for him. I have to get to the surface so he can rest in peace. I kick against the bottom of the lake and try to mermaid swim to the top. The ropes are holding me down especially since I can't use my arms. Then I see him. Josh. He swims toward me and looks sadly at my bound wrists and ankles. I hope he's here to help me, but from the look on his face, I can tell I may only have a couple of minutes, maybe less. This is it. This is how Autumn Marie Fisher Parker Dies. Widowed. Childless. Drowned at the bottom of a lake.

A lump grows in my throat as I close my eyes. My lungs are giving out and I can feel my body growing heavy. I'm so tired. Maybe I should sit down. My head falls forward and I let go. Let go of this life. My hopes. My dreams. Everything I've ever wanted because it's over. I'm done for. Maybe Travis will find my body some day before the fish consume it all. My parents will be devastated. I hope Travis finds love again and Cat gets a great stepmom. Everything starts to go dark then I'm moving. Someone's pulling me upward, but I don't have the strength to open my eyes. When we reach the surface, I can feel the sun on my face and people yelling, but they seem so far away.

"Get her out! Is she breathing?"

Water splashes around me as someone drags me to the side of the pond. I still can't open my eyes. My lungs are on fire. I try to breathe, but something feels stuck. Someone's mouth covers mine and I feel air seep into my lungs. I begin to cough then I'm turned onto my side. Water spills from my mouth and I gasp for air.

"Oh, thank God," Travis says, rubbing my back.

I take a few more breaths before the paramedics descend upon me and begin to check me out. Questions are thrown at me so fast I can barely nod in response.

"Let's give her some space," Travis orders, taking my hand as I'm loaded onto a stretcher. He smiles down at me. "I'm so glad you're alright."

"How did you know where to find me?" I cough out.

He shakes his head. "I was driving out here to make sure everyone checked out of the inn and things were locked up. I saw the tip of the shack sinking and got the strangest feeling you were inside." He gulps like it's painful for him to talk about. "I called the hospital and when they said you were missing, I just knew you were in there." He kisses my hand as I'm loaded into the ambulance. "Who did this to you?"

"I-I don't know. Someone opened the door before they cut the shack off the dock, but they stood in the shadows." The hairs on the back of my neck stand up and I feel like someone's watching me. I glance over Travis's shoulder and that's when I spot them. It's when I know who did this. "Travis, I know who killed Sloan."

He furrows his brow. "Autumn..."

"No, listen to me. I know everything in the hospital I told you sounds crazy, but how else would I know Mr. Gillman was at the bottom of the lake?"

Travis pulls on the back of his neck. "Yeah, I saw his body. I'll have a diver extract it."

"Did you question Mr. and Mrs. Soggs about it?"

He shakes his head. "Mr. Soggs was released while you were in surgery. By the time you told me everything, they were gone. We have an APB out on them, but the chances of finding them are pretty slim. I looked them up. They're good about flying under the radar especially with Mrs. Soggs's... I mean Mrs. Sonia Rademan's make-up skills. Soggs was an alias." He sighs. "I'm not sure we'll ever find them."

I listen to what he tells me while still keeping my eyes on Sloan's killer and my attempted murderer. "Has everyone else left?"

"Not yet, Olive, George and Anita are packing up. They'll be heading out before long. I can't say I'm sad to see them go. This whole weekend was a disaster. Inviting strangers into this town was not good for Daysville."

"Why did you let Olive out?" I say, watching the killer interact with one of the officers.

"Well that was the judge's doing. Olive doesn't have a record and he thought the stress of the weekend had more to do with the attack then anything. Since Paula is well... dead and can't press charges, he let her go."

I nod.

"Autumn, what are you staring at? Are you feeling okay?" He glances to the paramedic. "We need to get her back to the hospital. She just had brain surgery and almost drowned. What's taking so long?"

Before the paramedic can respond, I squeeze Travis's hand. "I'm not ready to go quite yet."

He frowns. "What do you mean?"

"I mean I know who killed Sloan and who just tried to kill me."

"You do? Who? I thought you didn't see them."

"I didn't, but I-I just know."

"Did you get a vision?" His face is etched with concern.

I shake my head. "Call it instinct."

He studies me for a moment then says, "Autumn, you have to have proof. We can't just accuse someone of killing Sloan and attempting to kill you."

"I'm pretty sure I can get a confession."

"Autumn," he groans.

I pat his hand. "Please let me try."

"Fine." Then he mumbles under his breath, "I'm going to regret this."

I smirk at him then gesture to the officer. "Call him over."

He cocks his eyebrow at me, but does as I ask.

I'm pleased that the killer comes with him.

"What's up boss?" The officer asks, shooting me a sympathetic look.

Travis steps out of the ambulance and pulls the officer off to the side to give me some privacy. Although he doesn't go too far.

The paramedic raises an eyebrow at me then says, "I'm going to check with the driver to see if we're ready to go. I'll be right back."

I nod my thanks then turn to the killer. "Are you ready to get back home?"

They give me a fake smile. "Definitely. It's been a long weekend to say the least. I'm ready for some normalcy." They pause and study me, probably trying to gauge whether or not I recognize them as my kidnapper/attempted murderer. "How are you feeling?"

"Glad to be alive." I give them a closed lipped smile then ask, "What are your plans moving forward?"

"Oh, you know, get back to work. See clients, advertise, go home, repeat."

"Hmm. Sounds like my life."

They laugh. "Tis the life of a massage therapist."

I snort. "A dedicated one that's for sure."

They smile.

"How do you plan to live with yourself?"

Their smile falters. "Wh-what do you mean?"

"I mean you killed Sloan and tried to kill me. A person doesn't just go back to their life and forget all of that."

"I-I don't know what you're talking about." They glance toward Travis to see if he heard what I said. "You must not be feeling well. I'm going to get the paramedic. You need to get back to the hospital and rest. You're not thinking straight. Paula killed Tony and Sloan. That's what Mr. Gillman said. He said she admitted to it."

"Oh, you mean Mr. Soggs or Mr. Rademan, whatever his name is. The real Mr. Gillman's dead."

They gasp. "No, that can't be. We just saw him and Mrs. Soggs about an hour ago. They said they were going to take a drive and to let ourselves out."

"That wasn't the real Mr. Gillman or Mrs. Soggs. Those were two con artists who kept the money they stole from people at the inn so no one could find it if they ever got caught."

"No way."

I nod.

"Wow. That's crazy... but Paula still confessed to killing Tony and Sloan."

"Did she?"

They furrow their brow.

"Paula overheard Mr. and Mrs. Soggs or the Rademan's talking about killing Mr. Gillman and about all the money they stole. That's why they killed her. She never confessed to anything, but you already know that. So why did you lie?"

"I-I didn't. That's what they told me."

"So, you didn't actually hear Paula confess?"

"Well no."

"And Paula didn't try to attack anyone, did she?"

Their face grows red and they ball their fists. "It's our word against yours. You weren't even there."

"No, I wasn't, but I talked to someone who was."

Realization spreads across their face and their eyes dart toward their vehicle.

I know I have them right where I want them. I just need them to confess because otherwise I have no proof and essentially no case. "Sloan admitted to killing Tony. They were half-brothers. Both of them were con artists just like their parents, but you already knew that, didn't you?"

"How do you... who? Sloan told you? When?"

I shrug. "Doesn't matter. The fact is I know he killed Tony and Paula told me she didn't kill Sloan."

"And you believe her?"

"Pretty sure she has no reason to lie to me when she's dead."

Their eyes widen. "De-dead? As in you talked to her ghost."

I nod. "Hers, Mr. Gillman's, Tony's and even Sloan's."

"S-so Sloan told you who killed him. How could he know? He was facing the window when I..." Their voice trails off when they realize what they said.

I smile. "And why did you try to kill me?"

Their eyes narrow. "Because I knew you would figure it out. You see things... visions. I thought maybe you saw something before you left for the hospital. I didn't want to take any chances."

"Why did you do it? Why did you kill Sloan?"

They laugh loudly.

Travis and the officer shift closer to us sensing something's about to go down.

That's when they pull a gun from behind their back and point it at me.

18

"Nobody move or I'll shoot her."

Travis has one hand on his gun and another out in front of him as if he can stop them from shooting me. "Let's just take a minute. Everyone take a breath. What's going on here?"

"What's going on is I'm leaving and no one's going to follow me. No one's going to come after me. Got it?" They back away from the ambulance, but the gun is still pointed at my chest as they inch their way to their car. "I mean it. I'll kill her."

Travis nods, but keeps his eyes trained on them.

My heart's beating so fast I can hardly breathe. From the look in their eyes, I know they will kill me and not even think twice about it.

A truck roars into the driveway, crashing into their car and knocking them down in the process.

Everything happens at lightning speed. Police officers swarm the truck and pull the driver from the driver's seat. Travis lunges for the suspect before they can attempt to get up and run. When he pulls them up, they lock eyes with me and smirk.

"I killed Sloan because he double crossed me."

"What?"

Travis cuffs them, reads them their rights then walks them over to me.

"How did Sloan double cross you, George?"

George glares at me. "Sloan was my best friend. We've been conning people since we were teenagers. His parents got us into the business. I met Anita at a bar and found out she was rich. She was going to massage school at the time so I enrolled. Sloan and Tony enrolled too. It turns out a lot of trust fund kids try to find themselves by taking these kinds of certification courses." He rolls his eyes.

I lift an eyebrow. "So, you, Sloan and Tony decided to become massage therapists in hopes of finding targets to con?"

George shrugs. "It worked, didn't it? I got Anita to marry me."

"But Tony tried to pursue her?"

George hangs his head. "Yeah, he did that because I fell in love. I wanted to get out of the business and build a life with Anita. Tony and Sloan didn't take it well and neither did their parents. They threatened to expose me to Anita if I didn't go along with their claim that Paula tried to attack Anita and they had to shoot her in self-defense." He shakes his head in disgust. "Tony wanted to punish me for falling in love by trying to steal Anita from me. Prove that she didn't really love me. He tried and failed and was planning to try again. Expose me to Anita or even try to get me to cheat on her then marry her only to divorce her and run off with Paula, leaving us all high and dry. I overheard Sloan and

Tony arguing about it when we got back to the inn that first night."

"And you didn't confront them?"

George shakes his head. "No, they would have killed me. If I was dead, who would protect Anita?" He hangs his head then mumbles, "Sloan must have decided to get rid of Tony then take me out so he would be the only one left to comfort Anita. I wasn't about to let that happen."

Anita gasps behind him. Tears spill down her cheeks. "So, I was nothing more than a cash cow?"

George turns to look over his shoulder at her. "No, babe. It's not like that. I love you."

Anita bursts into tears, spins on her heels and takes off for the inn.

George calls after her, but she slams the door in response. He drops his head in defeat as Travis hands him off to another officer.

Travis smiles at me. "Well I guess your gut instinct was right."

I shrug. "Nah, I knew Olive and Anita couldn't have carried me from the hospital and they certainly couldn't have sawed the shack off the dock." I shake my head and add, "The hospital really needs to get that emergency door fixed. It's a liability."

Travis chuckles. "I'll get right on that." Then he sighs. "Well Miss Fisher, I guess you've solved another mystery. And you didn't even need your visions to do so."

I look down at my hands and blink back the tears threatening to spill over.

"Hey, Aut. What's wrong?" Travis jumps up into the ambulance.

"No-nothing," I croak then sniffle.

"Aut, look at me," he says, softly.

I shake my head.

He tugs on my chin so I'm forced to look at him. "You don't need those visions to be a good sleuth. You've solved many cases by simply following clues and asking questions. You'll still be able to do that."

"It's not that," I sniffle again.

"Then what?"

I chew on my lip not wanting to tell him why not seeing visions anymore is bothering me. I know I can solve cases without them.

"It's Josh, isn't it?" Travis whispers, running a hand through his hair.

My heart aches hearing Josh's name. "I'm never going to see him again," my voice cracks.

Travis closes his eyes and gulps like hearing me say those words physically causes him pain. When he opens his eyes I only see sympathy, not hurt or jealousy. "I know, Aut and I wish I could bring him back for you. He was your best friend... your hu-husband." He gulps again at those words. "You must really miss him."

I nod and burst into tears.

Travis wraps his arms around me and holds me while I cry. His woodsy scent fills my nose and somehow soothes me. "I'm so sorry, Aut."

Someone clears their throat behind us. "Excuse me, Captain, but I need to talk to you."

I wipe my eyes and look up at the officer standing in front of us.

Travis squeezes my hand and studies me as if to determine if I'm okay.

I force a smile and nod toward the officer.

"I'll be right back," he says, then jumps out of the ambulance.

I watch as the two head toward the truck that crashed into George's car. The driver's surrounded by cops so I can't see his face.

Travis talks to the guy for a minute then rushes back over to me.

"Who is that? What's going on?"

"Nothing. We need to get you back to the hospital." He pounds on the partition to get the paramedics attention.

"Travis, you're acting weird. Why are you in such a hurry?"

Travis ignores me and turns to the paramedic. "Take her directly to Dr. Gregory. He's waiting to check her out. Do not stop for anyone, do you understand me?"

I frown at his words. "Travis, talk to me. Tell me what's going on," I demand.

He kisses my forehead then jumps out of the ambulance and slams the doors.

The ambulance's sirens come on and the ambulance lunges forward.

I lean my head back on the stretcher, wondering why Travis ran off like he did. Who was in the truck?

The ambulance doesn't get far before it swerves, veering off to the right.

"What the... hey, what's going on?" the paramedic next to me yells to the driver.

"There's a truck. It's trying to run me off the road," the driver hollers back.

The ambulance moves to the left then back to the right before tires screech, metal crunches, glass breaks and we're thrown forward before coming to a stop.

I can smell smoke and gasoline. Not a good combo. I'm strapped into the stretcher and the paramedic next to me is groaning. Blood's dripping from a gash on his head and he seems disoriented. "Hey, we have to get out of here!"

He groans again and stumbles trying to gain his footing.

I make quick work of the buckles and free myself from the stretcher. Before either of us can open the doors, they miraculously open. Only the person standing on the other side of the door isn't someone I would call our knight in shining armor.

19

"Come with me," he orders.

I open my mouth to tell him no when I catch a whiff of smoke. This ambulance is going to go up in flames with us in it if we don't get moving.

The paramedic sways next to me. "Hey, I know you," he slurs. Blood spills down the side of his head and onto his shirt as he stumbles out of the ambulance. He falls into the grass, holding his head.

There's no movement from the front of the ambulance. I'm not sure what that means for the driver.

"Get out, Mrs. Parker."

I slowly make my way to the back of the ambulance, scanning the road for Travis. Where is he?

"He's not coming." He smirks. "At least not yet. Get in the truck."

I chew on my lip, pondering my options.

"Now, Mrs. Parker or I'll shoot them." He pulls a gun from behind his back and points it at the paramedic.

His eyes widen in surprise then send me a pleading look.

"Don't shoot. I'll go with you."

"Wise choice," he spouts, gesturing with the gun toward his truck. It's got front end damage from where he slammed into George's vehicle and some damage from hitting the ambulance. He pushes the gun into my ribs as we walk toward his truck.

I glance over my shoulder at the ambulance. Smoke's still billowing from the hood. The whole front end is smashed into a tree and the driver's slowly lifting his head from the steering wheel. I can hear sirens in the distance. Maybe if I stall...

"Move it, Mrs. Parker." He jabs the gun deeper into my ribs causing me to flinch.

He opens the driver's door and pushes me across the seat then gets in and slams the truck into drive. The tires squeal as he makes a U-turn and heads down a dirt path just off the two-lane road.

The lane is bumpy so I hang onto the handle to avoid hitting my head on the ceiling. Speaking of my head, it's throbbing. The bandage is soaked from the lake and I know it's not good for my stitches to be wet not to mention I'll probably end up with some sort of infection if it doesn't get treated soon. That is if I make it out of here alive.

"You know who I am, don't you?" he sneers next to me.

I straighten at his question and try to calm my racing heart. "You're the man who killed my husband."

"Ah, when did you figure it out?"

"When you opened the ambulance doors, I just knew. There was no other reason for you to be there. You killed Josh and came for me, right?"

He shakes his head with a smile playing on his lips. "Your husband made it so easy. Running out right in front of my truck. He and that dumb dog. It's like they were begging for me to hit them."

Bile boils up in my throat along with pure rage. I know he's trying to get a rise out of me, but I refuse to let him.

"You lied about the truck, Mr. Peterson."

He shoots me a smug smile. "Of course, I lied. I wasn't about to tell that captain it was my truck. I had to steer the attention off of me and onto someone else. Especially if Rivers ever decided to talk, which he won't if he knows what's good for him."

I mull over his words then ask, "What about the registration in the glove box?"

He laughs. "I pulled it from that drunk Danny's car. The internet makes it so easy to create false documents. A couple of clicks and a good scanner can do wonders."

I frown, my head throbbing and confusion taking over. "Why did you run into George's truck?"

"Who?"

"The guy at the inn. You ran into his car."

"Oh, he was holding a gun. I thought I'd help the police out."

I snort and roll my eyes. "My, what a good citizen you are. Why did they let you go?"

He smiles. "I told them I was test driving this truck and came to see my old friend Mr. Gillman when I saw that crazy guy holding a gun. I was simply doing my civil duty by protecting you and the police. They thanked me and sent me on my way."

"Really?"

He nods, looking rather pleased with himself. "They bought every word."

"So why were you really at the inn?"

"I have a police scanner and heard you were there. We needed to talk."

"Kidnap me is more like it," I mutter.

He huffs out a laugh. "That was the easy part. The police were busy tying up loose ends with the case. I told your lover boy captain that Josh's killer was after you so he needed to get you back to the hospital asap. It worked like a charm."

The lump in my throat makes it hard for me to speak, but I'm able to choke out, "Why?"

"Why? Why what?" He slides a glance over at me then smirks. "Ah, you want to know why I killed your husband?"

"Yes, why!" I scream, not even recognizing my own voice. "Why did you kill my best friend?" My voice cracks and I swallow the sob threatening to escape.

Frank grins again. "Now, Autumn. You really should be thanking me. I did you a favor."

"Wh-what?" I croak. "How is killing my husband doing me a favor?"

"Oh, Autumn. Don't you see the bigger picture?"

I blink, completely confused by his question.

He chuckles. "Here I thought you were some gifted sleuth, but you're not putting this mystery together at all."

I glare at him. "Because there isn't a mystery to solve here. You killed my husband because the captain ordered you to. You must have owed him money. He erases your debt by getting revenge on me, am I right?"

"Something like that."

"Why didn't he ask you to kill me?"

Frank mutters something I can't make out then says, "Why do you think I'm here now?"

"To kill me? Is that it?"

He doesn't respond, just turns up the radio to indicate our conversation is over. Luke Bryan's voice comes through the speakers and three margaritas and a shot sounds really good right now. We turn several more times before he pulls up in front of an old cabin. "Get out and don't even think about running off." Frank flings open the driver's door and hops out.

I push open the passenger side door and carefully step down. My head's throbbing and my stitches are itching like crazy. I need to get this bandage off.

"Hurry up, Mrs. Parker," Frank spats.

I tug at my bandage and rub my temples.

"What's the matter with you? Head hurting?"

"What do you think?" I snap, this day getting the best of me.

Frank shakes his head and motions with the gun toward the cabin.

I feel like I'm walking to my death. He's going to shoot me and leave my body here to rot. My legs feel like I've done a hundred squats as I trudge up the stairs. It's as if my body knows it's moments away from shutting down for good.

This is it.

This is how I die.

Today's the day.

It wasn't the brain tumor that got me. I didn't drown in the lake. Nope, it's being shot by the madman mechanic who killed my husband.

20

"Have a seat," Frank points to a lone wooden chair in the middle of the room.

I scan the one room cabin. There's a little kitchen tucked in the corner. A stone fireplace on the far wall and a single cot positioned along the wall by the door. "Is this your hunting cabin?"

"I don't hunt... at least not animals," he whispers in my ear.

Goosebumps form on my skin and a chill runs down my spine. I shiver at his words.

"Do I frighten you, Autumn?"

I swallow the lump in my throat and square my shoulders. *Don't show any signs of fear... right?* The paramedics have probably notified Travis by now so it shouldn't take him long to find me. Although the off road we took did have a lot of twists and turns. Maybe Travis won't be able to find me. I chew on my lip and fight the urge to cry.

"Sit."

"I'm not a dog," I mutter back.

"Sit down, Autumn. I won't ask again," he says, pressing the gun into my hip.

I force my legs to move and lower down into the chair. "What now?"

"We wait."

I furrow my brow. "Wait for what?"

He gives me a sly smile, not answering my question then moves to the kitchen.

Pots and pans clang together behind me, causing me to jump. Frank laughs loudly. "Did I scare you?"

I ignore him and look down at my hands.

Tires crunch in the driveway and a car door slams. My heart rate kicks up in my chest. I pray it's Travis who's come to save me, but as the seconds tick by into minutes, I know it's not him. He would have barged in here by now. A hollow feeling starts in the pit of my stomach. Whoever's outside is going to decide my fate and I know it's not going to be good.

A pop sounds outside followed by breaking glass and Frank falls to the floor.

My eyes widen in horror when I realize what just happened. Someone killed Frank and I'm probably next. I dive to the floor, feeling like it's my only hope. The cot's along the wall. I think about crawling underneath it, but what if they start shooting up the entire cabin, I'll be hit. I stay where I am and wait. I feel like a sitting duck. Just waiting for my fate. Waiting for my life to end.

Then the car door opens again, tires crunch on the gravel and eventually fade. I blink, wondering what just happened. Why didn't they come inside? Why would they kill Frank and leave me here?

I sit up slowly and crawl to the door. Is this a trick? Are they going to park somewhere and then come back for me? My heart pounds against my ribcage, like it wants to burst out. I reach for the door knob, take a deep breath then yank it open. I close my eyes and wait for something to happen. When nothing does, I open them and make my way onto the porch.

The sun's fading behind the clouds and the air's still hot like a storm's getting ready to roll in although we haven't seen rain in days. I glance around, my eyes falling on Frank's truck. It's my only way out of here although I have no idea where I am.

Luckily, he left the keys inside because digging them out of a dead man's pocket doesn't appeal to me. I search around for a phone to call Travis, but come up empty. How does someone not have a phone? Maybe he kept it in his pocket, but I think twice before attempting to find it. I can find my way back to town without... I think.

I turn on the truck, put it in gear then glance around one last time.

The woods are eerily quiet. No birds chirping, no squirrels running around. Nothing. The hairs on the back of my neck stand up and I get the strange feeling I'm being watched. I throw the truck into drive and spin out on the road. I don't make it far before a loud boom erupts behind me.

My eyes flick to the rearview mirror where there's smoke and flames engulfing the cabin. If I would have waited only a few minutes longer I would be dead right now. The thought turns my stomach as I push down harder on the gas pedal. My eyes dart around the woods looking for any sign of danger or really any sign that will lead me back to town.

When I break through the clearing, I spot a black sedan idling by the side of the road. The driver's leaning against it with a cigarette in his hand and what looks like a device in the other. My heart kicks back up in my chest and my intuition tells me this is the man who killed Frank and blew up the cabin.

Before I can do anything, he spots me and scrambles around to the driver's side of his car. I stomp on the gas and drive in the opposite direction. It doesn't take long for him to catch up to me. The road's bumpy and full of pot holes. I'm thankful I have a truck, but unfortunately, the guy behind me is keeping up quite well. I make a sharp turn, praying he misses it, but my heart sinks when he doesn't. Another turn comes along and I floor the gas, the engine groans in protest, but doesn't give out on me. At that moment, the sky opens up and rain pours down from the sky. *Great. Just great. I really don't need this right now.* I flick on the wipers and squint my eyes to try and see through the downpour.

After a few more turns, I think I've lost the guy and see blacktop ahead. My heart soars and I know once I hit the pavement, I'll be able to get back to town. The sound of tires screeching as I turn onto the pavement has me doing a double take. I swerve out of the way before the sedan can hit me. A gun is out the window of the sedan and the driver pops off a few rounds. I slam the truck into reverse and press my foot on the gas. Going backwards, away from this madman. When the sedan realizes I'm not following him, he stops and has to turn around. It also gives me the chance to do the same then I'm heading north and praying there's a sign for Daysville before he can catch up to me.

Another pop sounds behind me and I duck down just in case he takes out the back window, but the sound of breaking glass never comes. I push down harder on the gas and almost miss the sign that says, *Welcome to Daysville.* I don't think I've ever been more excited to see that sign in my entire life. The tires squeal and the bed of the truck fishtails as I make the turn toward Daysville.

A horn blares behind me, causing me to jump. The guy's riding my bumper and honking his horn, waving at me to pull over. Yeah, that's not going to happen. Another pop sounds and the truck swerves to the left, followed by a hissing sound. A thumping sound comes from the rear. The guy shot out my tire. I try not to panic. We're still a couple of miles outside of town and if he shoots all of my tires... I gulp and grip the steering wheel even tighter. The truck whines as I stomp down on the gas. *Please don't fail me now. Not when I'm this close. This close to town. To safety. To Travis.*

The realization hits me like a punch to the stomach, almost knocking the wind out of me. Travis. It's always been Travis. He's the one. The one who rescues me when I'm in danger. The one I call when I need help. The one who's there when I need him... until I shut him out. I close my eyes for only a second when I realize I'm the one who kept us from being together all these years. When I open my eyes, I see it.

Not the stretch of road that leads into Daysville although it is in front of me. No, our life or what could have been our life. If I'd forgiven Travis. If I'd listened to his explanation. If I'd fought for our love. If I'd not been so stubborn. We would have had a life with babies. With Cat as my daughter. We could have raised her together. Fought April for custody or at the very least shared custody. We would be married. Solving cases while changing diapers. Laughing. Loving. Being Traut. I choke out a laugh at the ridiculous couple name Travis came up with when I gushed about Jen and Ben's cute couple name. I blink and realize I missed out on a life of great love and happiness because I let one night... one awful night of misunderstandings, anger, and hurt stand in the way of something great. I know deep down Travis would never betray me like that again. Heck the man hasn't even dated anyone seriously since high school. I guess you could count Allison, but I'm not sure Travis would. He's never fallen in love with anyone else. It's always been me and I know it always will be. He'll always by my hero, my protector, my rock and my love. Those last words sink into my heart. Taking all the brokenness. The hurt. The pain. The betrayal. Even the hate and slowly stitching it back together.

There will always be a scar no matter how hard I try to erase it, but scars aren't always bad. They're a reminder of everything we've been through. The good, the bad and the ugly. Those three things define my relationship with Travis. When I was young and naïve, I didn't realize forgiveness was an option. I simply let my heart grow cold. Closed off to anyone and everything until Josh thawed it. He taught me I could love again, trust again, be happy again but it wasn't the encompassing love I had with Travis. I've never loved anyone like I loved Travis... and I never will.

Metal scraping on the pavement jerks me back to the present. I can smell burning rubber and know it's the rim causing the noise. It's only a matter of time before I won't be able to keep going. I see the church steeple and know I'm getting close, but I'm not sure I'm going to make it. The police station's downtown. Travis is there. I have to get to him. I have to tell him how I feel. I can't die, not like this. Not when I've finally found my way back home. My home is with him. Him and Cat. They're my family.

Butterflies erupt in my stomach just thinking about it. I glance down at my stomach and imagine it round and swollen with our twins. Our twins. Tears fill my eyes as a vision fills my head. A boy and a girl with beautiful red hair, freckles dotting their noses, laughing as Travis chases them around the yard. While I watch from the porch with my arm around Cat. Our family.

The sound of metal on metal causes me to cringe. I'm jolted forward, hitting my head on the steering wheel, pain shoots across my forehead. Another hit and more pain. This can't be good for my brain. I mean, I literally just got out of surgery yesterday. The guy rams into the truck again then there's another pop and I feel the front tire go out and the hiss of the radiator. Smoke begins to billow out from the hood. My mind races with what to do.

The church is coming into view and I see a couple people standing underneath umbrellas in the graveyard. An idea forms in my mind and I lean on the horn. They whip their heads around just as the truck clunks and heaves before coming to a stop. I keep leaning on the horn and praying they come to my rescue.

My heart's pounding so loud in my ears that it almost drowns out the sound of the horn. I'm not sure if I should try to get out and make a run for it or not. I feel weak. So tired. My head's throbbing and I almost feel like I may pass out. Maybe if I just close my eyes for a minute. I put my head down on the steering wheel as the horn fizzles out, sounding like a deflating balloon. This is it, I sigh and wait for what happens next.

21

"Autumn, wake-up."

I groan and flinch because it feels like someone's playing cymbals in my head. A bright light is shining in my eyes for the second time today. "Am I dead?"

"No, you're at the hospital."

I blink then blink again before my eyes focus on a blond nurse checking my pulse.

"How are you feeling?"

"Like a band of percussionists are playing a concert in my head."

"That should pass soon." She pats my hand. "Your family is beside themselves waiting to see you. We've kept them at bay as long as we could, but they're growing restless. The doctor wanted you to get some rest. You've been through a lot since your surgery."

I snort because that's the understatement of the century. Seeing dead people, surviving brain surgery, being kidnapped from the hospital, almost drowning in a lake, being kidnapped again, tossed in a cabin, being shot at, almost blown up, then chased and shot at again not to mention the car crash and hitting my head on the steering wheel. I feel like I have whiplash just thinking about it all.

"Is she awake yet?" My mother pokes her head in the door with my father right behind her. They don't wait for the nurse to answer before they push their way into my room and engulf me in hugs. "We were so worried. How are you? Does anything hurt? Should I call the doctor?"

"I'm fine," I assure them then look toward the door, hoping Travis is right behind them. When the doorway's empty, I frown. I figured he'd be the first one in here.

"Is she up?" Josh's parents ask, coming into the room, followed by Cat and Regina who have their arms filled with balloons and flowers. Everyone fusses over me. Each of them talking over each other, asking how I'm feeling. I smile and nod, answer their questions and pretend to not feel like a lead weight is sitting on my chest. It feels so tight. Where is Travis? Did something happen? Is he ok? There's no other reason for him not to be here, right? Then dread fills me and my smile slips. What if he's... I choke and have a hard time catching my breath.

My mother calls for a nurse, who rushes in and slips an oxygen mask over my head.

"Deep breaths. Take a slow deep breath" Then she turns to everyone in the room and orders for them to get out. "You're overwhelming her. She needs her rest," she barks.

My parents' faces are etched with worry along with Josh's parents, Regina's and Cat's.

I lift a hand in a wave to try and assure them I'm fine, but I can tell they don't buy it.

They wave and blow kisses before leaving the room.

When my breathing returns to normal, the nurse takes the mask off my face. "Better?"

I nod.

"Family can be too much sometimes."

I nod again because my throat feels thick and my chest still hasn't loosened its vice grip on my lungs yet.

"I bet I have something that will cheer you up." She taps me on the shoulder then disappears out the door.

If she thinks ice cream or some stupid popsicle is going to take this lead weight off my chest she's crazy. The only thing that will make this better is...

"Hi, Aut."

My eyes flicker to the door and instantly I can breathe. "Trav," I breathe out his name then blink to make sure I'm not imagining it. "You're here."

He furrows his brow. "Where else would I be?" Tears fill my eyes and he's at my side in an instant, brushing them away. "Aut, what's wrong?"

I choke out a sob and shake my head.

"You thought something happened to me, didn't you?" He takes my hands in his and rubs his thumbs over my knuckles. "Because I'm usually here when you wake-up, right?"

Another sob escapes my mouth and I nod.

He kisses my forehead. "I had some loose ends to tie up at the station, but I got here as quickly as I could. I figured you'd be sleeping a little longer. Guess I underestimated you." He winks at me.

I smile then ask, "Wh-what happened?"

His green eyes grow dark. "You mean after you passed out?"

"Yeah." I gulp, wondering if I really want to hear it, but I know my curiosity will get the best of me.

He smirks. "Lucky for you, the acting captain of the police department was cruising down the street, looking everywhere for this cute sleuth who tends to get herself into some rather dangerous situations. He heard her honking and quickly rushed to save her. When he found her unconscious, he nearly had a heart attack."

I squeeze his hand and shoot him a shy smile. "Then what happened?"

"Well before he saved her, he had to take down the bad guy."

"Who was?"

"One of River's goons. Remember the guy that Frank told us the truck that ki-..." he clears his throat. "Anyway, remember the guy he said it belonged too?"

I nod. "Daniel Myers."

"Yes."

"That was Daniel Myers?"

Travis nods. "Seems the old captain ordered him to take out Frank and tie up loose ends."

"I was a loose end?"

"I guess so." Travis runs his thumb over my knuckles again. "He's in jail now. He'll be there for a long time."

I chew on my lip, processing everything Travis just told me. "Do you think the captain will ever give up on trying to hurt me? Will he try to hurt you? Cat?" I squeak out. My heart kicking up at the thought and the monitor starts beeping wildly next to me.

"Hey, hey, Aut. Breathe. Take a deep breath." He tips my chin so I'm forced to look at him. "You're safe. I'm safe. Cat's safe. No one's ever going to hurt you or Cat, okay? You girls are my life. I'll die protecting you and even then, I'll come back and protect you just like Josh did."

Tears form in my eyes as I take a deep breath and I try to blink them away.

Travis tilts his head and studies me. "Talk to me. What's

going on in that pretty head of yours? Is it this case? The surgery? Josh?"

Before I can answer there's a knock at the door.

"Excuse me, Captain. I need to check out our patient," Dr. Gregory says, stepping into the room. "Also, the station called saying they've been trying to get a hold of you. Seems your phone is turned off. It sounds important."

Travis checks his phone. "Shoot. I forgot I silenced it." He fixes his gaze back on me and looks conflicted. "I'm sorry."

"It's fine. Go. You're the captain. The town needs you." I squeeze his hand to re-assure him.

He still looks torn up about leaving me as he squeezes my hand back then stands. "I won't be long."

I smile at him then watch him leave the room.

Dr. Gregory lifts an eyebrow at me when my gaze finally lands on him, but he doesn't say anything. He proceeds to check my stitches and ask me questions.

I do my best to answer them all while keeping an eye on the door. Where is Travis? Did something else happen? I fidget with the blanket and Dr. Gregory takes it as a sign I'm antsy to get out of here.

"I wanted to keep you here a few more days for observation, but your mother thinks you'll rest better at home. Not to mention she thinks you'll be safer. She's threatening to sue the hospital after you were kidnapped." He sighs and jots something else down in his notes. "I can't say I blame her so we agreed to a compromise." Before I can ask about the compromise, he continues, "A nurse will come to your house a couple of times a day to check in on you. Check your stitches, change the bandage, help you wash your hair, monitor your pain medication, that sort of thing."

I balk at his words. "I'm fine. I don't need a nurse."

He smirks. "I'll let you take that up with your mother. This is non-negotiable for me so just please let us take care of you."

"Fine," I pout, crossing my arms over my chest.

"Good girl," he pats my arm. "I'm headed back to Chicago tonight, but feel free to call me if you have any questions. I'll be back in town for your six-week check-up. In the meantime, try to take it easy. No more cases. No more kidnappings, guns blazing craziness okay?"

I huff like it's really going to be a hardship. "I'll try." Then I smile and say, "Thanks doc."

He winks at me. "Take care of yourself, Autumn."

"You too." I watch him leave and wait for Travis to come back in. Within minutes, my parents along with Josh's are in my room, helping me get ready to leave. "Where's Travis?"

They all exchange curious glances then my mother pipes up, "He had to go back to the station. It seems there was an incident."

I frown at her words. "Incident? What kind of incident?"

My mother pats my hand. "Nothing for you to worry about dear. Now, let's get you home."

22

"I love you and I always will. You're my best friend," I sniff as I pour Josh's ashes around the base of our tree. The one we carved our initials in as kids then again after we got married. I look around at Josh's parents and mine who are all wiping their tears with Kleenex as they say their final good-bye-'s.

It's been a week since I've been out of the hospital and the nurse allowed me to venture out into the woods to scatter Josh's ashes. Our parents are heading back to Florida today at my insistence. They've been hovering all week and I can barely breathe. I told them the best medicine would be for me not to have to worry about them and to think of them relaxing by the beach. They all protested and my mother is still trying to find ways to stay, but I sat my father down and told him I needed some space. He reluctantly agreed and talked everyone else into it too.

I swipe at the tears then force a smile at all of them. "Thank you for being such great parents, mentors and friends. Josh and I love you all so much."

They surround me in seconds with hugs, tears and goodbyes. Then they each give me one last hug before retreating to the house to head out.

I watch them leave then turn back to our tree, running my hand over our initials. "I miss you, Josh. I'll never forget you." I kiss my fingertips then hold them to the tree before I turn back to the house.

When I make my way through the clearing, I see Travis making his way toward me. His red hair's disheveled like he's been running his hand through it all day, his white button-down shirt is slightly wrinkled along with his slate gray pants. His shiny black shoes stand out in the grass as he stomps down the hill toward me.

His face lights up when he sees me. "Aut, I'm sorry. I wanted to be here for this. I got hung up at the station. I..."

Before he can fling another reason why he wasn't with me today, I press a finger to his lips to silence him and shake my head. "You're here now and that's all that matters."

He blinks like he's not sure he heard me correctly. "But I-" he murmurs against my finger.

"Nope. Doesn't matter."

"Aut, I-"

I remove my finger from his lips. "Travis, you're the acting captain of Daysville. You have cases. Staff. Obligations. The people of this town are depending on you. Plus, you've been swamped all week with some secret incident that everyone's gossiping about."

He opens his mouth to say something and I press my finger to his lips again.

"Today wasn't something you needed to attend. It was about me, my parents and Josh's parents saying good-bye to Josh. Putting him to rest. I appreciate that you wanted to be here for me, but I understand. It's okay."

He doesn't say anything for a few moments then clears his throat. "Can I speak now?"

I smile. "Sure, go ahead."

He grins and gestures toward the house. "Care to go inside where it's cool?"

I nod, already feeling my flowery maxi dress sticking to my back. It was Josh's favorite so I knew I had to wear it today. I hold onto the edge of the skirt as we trek up the hill with Travis's assistance. Neither of us say anything until we reach my front porch. I notice my parents' and Josh's cars are gone. I breathe a sigh of relief, knowing they won't be hovering around me for the next five weeks. Now if I can just get rid of the bossy nurse. Luckily, she's gone for the day. I had her come early to check on me then told her to take the night off because I knew I'd want to be alone. Although now that Travis is here, I don't really feel like being by myself.

He holds open the front door for me. We both groan as the cold air hits us. "It's not even July and it's almost a hundred degrees."

I nod in agreement. "Ice tea?"

"I'll get it," he moves to head to the kitchen.

"No. Sit. You've been working all day. I'll get it."

He looks unsure.

"Sit, Trav. I'll get it. It's tea not a five-course meal."

"Fine," he sighs and plops down on the couch.

I hurry to the kitchen, grabbing the pitcher of tea from the fridge and two glasses along with some fresh watermelon then throw it on a tray and join Travis in the living room. He's staring at the fireplace although it's not on. He looks like he's a million miles away, with his right foot crossed over his knee. His left one's bouncing up and down like he's nervous about something.

When Travis spots me, he jumps to his feet, grabbing the pitcher. "Here, I'll pour."

I eye him suspiciously then flop down on the couch. "What's wrong? You're fidgeting. You only do that when there's something you need to tell me, but don't want to."

Handing me a glass, he doesn't meet my eyes then sits down next to me.

"Thanks," I say, taking it then tucking my legs underneath me on the couch. "Trav, what is it?" My heart thumps loudly in my chest and I try to calm it by taking a deep breath, but it doesn't do any good. I'm practically about to burst out of my skin waiting for him to say something. Anything. I take a drink to soothe my nerves.

He takes a long drink before setting the glass on a coaster. Then he turns to me and says something I'm not expecting. "Daniel Myers and Captain Rivers are dead."

I'm mid sip when he tells me this and I begin choking on my tea. He pats my back and takes the glass from my hand. When I finally catch my breath I choke out, "Wh-what? How? When?"

Travis sighs and runs a hand over his face. The bags and circles under his eyes show his exhaustion. His shoulders slump forward and he rests his elbows on his knees. He rolls his neck from side to side then rubs the back of it.

"What's wrong with your neck?"

"Nothing. Just tight. Probably slept on it wrong."

"Or you're completely stressed out." I point to the floor in front of me. "Come on, I'll rub your shoulders."

"No, Aut. I'm fine. Really."

I lift an eyebrow at him and motion to the floor. "Don't fight me on this, Trav. Sit."

He huffs out a breath like I'm making him scrub the toilets, but he plops down in front me. "This really isn't necessary, Aut," then he groans when I dig into his traps. "Oh, that feels... yeah right there." He moans again.

I smirk and work on his shoulders and neck in silence for a while, letting him fully relax before I press for more information about the deaths.

"Aut, that feels so good. You have magical hands," Travis murmurs, his words slurring like he's in utter bliss.

"I've been told that a time or two, but it's always good to hear," I whisper in his ear before finishing his shoulder massage with a sweeping move to clear the energy.

Travis leans his head back in my lap, his eyes closed and he looks about half asleep. So, when he speaks, I start a little at his voice, "They found both of them in their cells. They hung themselves."

"Hung themselves?" I blink and try to wrap my head around all of this. "I don't know Daniel, but that doesn't seem like something the powerful and arrogant Captain Rivers would do."

"I know. That's what I've been trying to figure out all week."

"Did they leave a note?"

"Daniel didn't, but Rivers did. Confessed to all the crimes. Even some we didn't know about. It all seems too clean. Too cut and dry. I wonder if he's trying to protect someone or someone didn't want him talking."

"Did he have any visitors the day he died?"

Travis opens his eyes and lifts his head. Stretches and grunts as he pulls himself back up onto the couch. "His only visitor was Daniel Myers. That must have been when he gave him the order to kill Frank... and you."

I frown. "Frank's dead. Daniel's dead and the captain too." I tap my chin. "Do you think the captain was working for someone else in town?"

"Gosh, I hope not." Travis drops his head back on the couch and closes his eyes again.

I open my mouth to ask Travis another question when I hear deep breathing and light snores from his side of the couch. I sigh, grab a blanket from the back of the couch and cover him up. His phone beeps on the coffee table. Regina's name pops up along with a message asking when he's coming home. I reach for the phone and type out a quick text letting Regina know Travis fell asleep on my couch. She texts back immediately with a winking emoji. I send her back an eye roll emoji then put his phone back on the table. When I move to stand up, a hand grabs my wrist and I yelp.

"Hey, it's just me. Sorry, I fell asleep for a minute." Travis releases my wrist, scrubs his face then blinks a few times. "I should go. Regina's making dinner. I told her I was going to stop by here then I'd be home. I've been working non-stop trying to figure this out. I need to spend some time with Cat." Travis rubs his eyes. "Sorry, I'm rambling." He moves to stand up, but I stop him.

"You're a good man, Trav."

His eyes soften and he reaches up to stroke my cheek, but stops himself and lowers his hand back down. "Thanks, Aut. I want to be the man you deserve. The dad Cat deserves. That these babi-" he glances at my stomach then looks away and clears his throat. "I-"

I place my hand over his. "Travis look at me."

He turns his gaze to me and we lock eyes just as his phone rings.

Travis breaks eye contact to glance at his phone. "Shoot, it's the station." Then he gives me an apologetic smile before answering. "Captain Mills." He stands and moves to the kitchen.

I flop back on the couch not sure what exactly I was

going to say to him. Now, doesn't seem like the right time to tell him about my epiphany in Frank's truck. Spreading Josh's ashes today made his death final. I guess I've been holding on for fear of forgetting him. Forgetting what we had, but I know I'll never forget him. He was my best friend and always will be.

"Sorry about that. You looked like you wanted to say something and I definitely want to hear it, but I have to get back to the station. There's been a development."

I perk up at his words. "What kind of development?"

"Nothing concrete yet, but I have to go. I'm sorry." Travis studies me for a moment. "Do you need anything?" He sighs and rakes a hand through his hair. "I hate that I fell asleep on you. You probably wanted to talk about Josh. This day can't be easy for you. I want to be here for you. Really, I do." He sighs again.

Standing up quickly, I rush over to him. "Trav, it's fine. I'm fine. You have a job to do. I understand. Go. I need some time alone anyway."

"Are you sure?" He furrows his brow and shoots me an uncertain look.

"Absolutely." I reach up and brush a loose strand of his hair back into place. "Be careful and try to get some rest, okay? I worry about you working so hard."

He places his hand over mine and studies me. "Aut, are you sure you're okay? I'll try to finish up at the station as quick as I can and-"

I cover his mouth with my hand. "Trav, I'm good. Really. Go catch the bad guys."

He smirks and murmurs against my hand. "Call me if you need anything."

"I will." I drop my hand and smile at him.

Travis hesitates like he wants to say something else, his

gaze bouncing from my eyes to my lips before he clears his throat and heads to the door. "I'll call you later."

"Okay, but get some sleep first.

He smiles, nods and heads into the night.

I move to the window and watch him pull out of my driveway. A soft breeze catches my attention and I turn to find Josh standing in front of the fireplace. I blink, wondering if I'm imagining it then worry the tumor isn't completely gone. I shouldn't be seeing ghosts.

He grins. "You're fine, Autumn. One hundred percent healthy. I just wanted to say good-bye. It's time for me to move on and you too. I wish it wouldn't have taken a car chase and bullets flying at you to realize what I've known all along. Travis is the one for you. Always has been and always will be."

Tears blur my eyes and I choke out, "I'm sorry."

Josh shakes his head and is in my face instantly. "Don't be sorry. Be happy. That's all I've ever wanted for you. I love you, Autumn."

"I love you too, Josh."

He shoots me one last smile before saying, "Go be happy. Promise me."

I nod and blow him a kiss as he disappears.

A sob escapes me and I fall to the floor, clutching my heart. Tonight, I grieve my best friend and husband. Tomorrow, I'll start a new chapter.

The End.

A NOTE FROM THE AUTHOR

Thank you so much for reading, "Salt Scrubs & Strangers"!! I so appreciate your support. This book took some time to write. I wanted to give me and Autumn time to heal after Josh's death. I re-wrote it several times before I was content with where it was heading. When I started this book, I had the mindset that this was going to be the last book in the series. By the middle, I knew there was no way I could sum up Autumn's and Travis's budding relationship in one book. With that said, there will be more books in this series!! (Insert happy dance) I'm not sure if it will be two more books or four more books. I'm going to let the characters guide me so stay tuned for more of these crazy characters.

If you enjoyed this book, please consider leaving a review at the end. I love reading them. Whether they're good or bad, they make me a better writer, so thank you for taking the time to leave one.

"Couples Massage & Corpses" is slated for release in September.

Writing a book is a commitment and not something that

can be done alone. I have a few people to thank for helping me with this book.

Mariah Sinclair is the queen of Cozy Mystery Covers and I absolutely love her covers! Her work is incredible and I'm so thankful for her creative vision on this cover.

A huge shout out to Gem from Gem's Proofreading for being my eyes on this book. She is a joy to work with and efficient too.

My family is also amazing. They are so supportive of my writing. They call out character names when I need one, bring me food and drinks when I'm busy typing away and encourage me to follow my dreams. Without them, I would struggle. They're my rocks and I love them dearly.

Another huge thank you to you, my reader, I so appreciate you and your support. If you would like to follow me on social media. Here are the links: Facebook Instagram

Until next time...

Happy Reading,

Jenn

ABOUT THE AUTHOR

Jenn Cowan is the author of several genres and has pen names under Jenna Richert and J.R. Cowan. When she's not writing you can find her in her massage office working on clients, cooking up a storm in her kitchen, hitting her yoga mat, singing and dancing with her hubby at a concert, cheering on the sidelines for her kiddos or cozied up by the fire reading a good book. She loves a good mystery and a happily ever after.

OTHER BOOKS BY THE AUTHOR:

~A Cozy Spa Mystery Series~

Massage & Murder (Book 1)

Hot Stones & Homicides (Book 2)

Reflexology & Revenge (Book 3)

Facials & Fugitives (Book 4)

Chair Massage & Chaos (Book 5)

Manicures & Mischief (Book 6)

Aromatherapy & Arsenic (Book 7)

~Non-Fiction~

Massage Basics: A Step by Step Guide to at Home Massage

www.ingramcontent.com/pod-product-compliance
Lightning Source LLC
Chambersburg PA
CBHW072229150726
48002CB00005B/2003